THE FRUIT

OF

OUR GRIEF

WILLIAM M. WILLIAMS

ISBN: 979-8-218-44387-0

CONTENTS

CHAPTER 1

The vehicle jolted down the highway as Ethan's gazed into the endless darkness beyond the window. He stood witness to the giants of the forest, their presence casting a dark, ominous shadow over the land. In contrast, the grass seemed as shallow as a whisper, in comparison to the rustling trees. A bitter gust of wind stirred the leaves, scattering them in a moment of panic, as the car passed by. Despite the unforgiving elements, the branches tolerated the restlessness. Farther away, a family of birds flew near the wooded abyss. One of the tiny Caroline Chickadees slammed against the limb of a tree and crashed on the concrete. Fallen from heavenly grace laid a feathered corpse.

From the bushes emerged a fox, a harbinger of death, sniffing and scouring the air. The scavenger paused. Then cautiously, the feral creature crouched toward the ground. Its eyes fixated on the beaked victim. Next, it snatched the bird with bared fangs, tearing flesh, and cracking hollow bones. After the fox's unholy communion, it vanished into the bushes. The only traces of the kill were feathers and a bloody residue. A few miles down the road, a highway sign with the word *East* came into focus. In this case, the direction was toward Mississippi.

Ethan turned toward the driver. Kendra, his mother, head swayed in a rhythmic motion to the radio. Tied in a bun, her hair-- bopped, hopped, and hip rolled-- to "Formation" by Beyonce. Ethan observed as she shimmied in the seat. Somehow, she had the energy despite driving the whole trip. Ethan, a teen with a worn-out brown skin tone, found himself unable to lift his head. He began dozing off on the journey, now approaching a seven-hour drive.

They stopped at hotels along the way, but he wished they had taken a plane. His mom claimed they didn't have the money. Whereas Ethan knew this road trip, providing them what she called "quality time" together, was a scheme to force him to confess. Several times during the trip, his mother tried to sneak in a question about that winter. She echoed his therapist. With his counselor, Ethan's responses were minimal at best. During sessions, he'd stare at the counselor—

fidgeting. He avoided eye contact, gazing at the bleak walls until their appointment ended. Sometimes Ethan might attempt the exercises, most futile breathing techniques. Yet, none of it altered the past. He'd rather express his feelings on his own terms. Whereas his mother perceived his silence as a ticking time bomb, especially if he didn't tell her. Ethan assumed she had an unspoken desire to ward off the spirit of solitude that haunted her. Her silent struggles went unnoticed or disregarded by most of her friends. At first, her cleaning rituals didn't seem a concern. Until at the old house, she would sweep the grass, slaving to make the front yard perfect. Recently, she started wiping down the lamps at the hotels. He assumed it was her way of staying in control of the chaos. After she had no choice but to sell the house, she seemed more uptight than when— his father died. Her nervous tics, or what

Ethan referred to as her "demons", took more control. Possessing her to do abnormal things.

As Ethan watched his mother dancing to another song. She noticed his gaze and smiled with a perfect row of teeth. Flawless as they were, the sound of a broken record was behind them. With her eyes stabbing him, he predicted the question but couldn't stop the routine. Kendra turned down the radio.

"Want to talk about it?" She asked as she had done before.

"No." Ethan replied, tugging at his shirt. He looked out the window, gazing at the passing scenery.

"I miss him too. It's okay *not* to be okay."

"Yup," Ethan recoiled. Knowing within an hour they would have the same conversation again. Ethan assumed his mother sought her own answer, or a script he refused to follow.

# # #

The house was huge, not like a mansion, but had enough room to hold two more people. Unlike the rest of the houses in Mississippi, it had siding walls instead of old bricks. Rather than seeing a horse, like the one a few miles back, Ethan saw a sports car in the driveway, the latest Ferrari. As Kendra approached, Ethan saw the grim gate that enclosed the house. Unlike the neighboring homes, this place had cameras that stared back. Ethan shifted his gaze from the house, feeling as if unseen eyes were watching him. He wondered if this place would be his cage.

The security gates opened; and Julian, his uncle, and David, Julian's partner, were waiting by the front door. Ethan didn't know too much about his uncle because the man never kept in contact. His mom claimed his uncle was a private person, but still family. To Ethan, Uncle Julian, with a bald-fade and a suit, was a stranger; he only knew his uncle as the CEO of a health company. Next to his uncle was David, his partner of nine years. Like Uncle Julian, David was a mystery. Ethan's mother mentioned it was strange that Julian and David weren't married, or at least engaged. Since David had lived with Julian for about five years, Kendra assumed they were on schedule for marriage, even buying a ring for Julian to propose. Sometimes Ethan would eavesdrop when she called Uncle Julian. That's if his uncle responded to her calls. Even if he answered, it was as though she was the only person on the line. Most of the time, from what Ethan overheard, Uncle Julian didn't discuss his business, including his romantic life. Despite the lack of information, Kendra always praised David. Ethan didn't know either of them or pretend to, so he had no opinion. In fact, he would have rather been somewhere he felt comfortable— not with strangers.

Ethan noticed David's shirt was sand-colored like a beach. It complimented his waves, his short black hair. Ethan's mother described it as a breeze brushing against a pond. In his opinion, David resembled a modern hippie. David's pants were too loose, but clean. Meaning that he didn't dress homeless but had a relaxed fit. His clothes were the same as weirdos at earth day concerts. Better yet, David dressed like people at those coffee shops. The places with plants and man buns. In contrast, Uncle Julian wore a constricted suit which appeared tailored and luxurious. It seemed the fabric had never experienced filth as if dry cleaned weekly. Like his uncle's attire, the house appeared polished and sophisticated. At the front door, David leaned against the house, unbothered. While Uncle Julian stood rigid, a bit unnerving. Seeing that their guest was entering the driveway.

Kendra parked the car and stepped out. Without hesitation, David skipped to the trunk and grabbed their bags. Ethan sighed, shooting a glare at David, the stranger unloading their belongings. Ethan figured the man didn't know personal boundaries but appreciated the effort. Whereas for Uncle Julian, it took long enough but he helped bring the rest in the house.

As they stepped in, Ethan noticed the flooring, rich birch wood, which led to a staircase with a vintage railing— for his mother to deep clean. As Ethan watched her check for dust, he hoped she wouldn't break anything. The place was a bit old fashioned, fragile— not dusty, but that wouldn't stop her. She would disinfect all the expensive antiques and surfaces. Her gaze suggested she would start with the flooring. Above the floors, a silver chandelier hung which made the walls a golden tan. On the left side of the house was the dining room, with a warm luminosity, which merged into the kitchen. An island, with a marble countertop, was in the middle of the space that had more birch flooring. The wood floors led back to the staircase which then went to the living room. This part of the house had lounge couches, a brick fireplace, and a library of books. Next to the books was a bar stand with a sign that read, David's Fun Time. Above the bar was a glass case with different colored bottles, most likely expensive liquor. In other words, David was a hippie and a daytime alcoholic. Ethan wrote a mental note about his uncle's mysterious lover.

Ethan's attention returned to the entrance of the house. He watched as his mother ran to David and Uncle Julian with open arms. Without a doubt, her hair swung from joy as David embraced Kendra's love. Unlike his partner, Uncle Julian had stepped away. For a glimpse, his mother looked as if she was slapped in the face. She stepped back, a reaction that seemed irritated and hurt. She huffed, spreading her arms out, again, toward Uncle Julian. Yet, his uncle raised a brow, staring at her from afar. Ethan knew she pretended to be okay, but his uncle's gesture had stung her. Meanwhile, Uncle Julian stepped around her and walked up the stairs. His uncle grabbed some bags and tossed their belongings into the rooms. Ethan noticed their host, Uncle Julian, chose bedrooms farthest away from the office. From down the hall, his uncle announced he didn't want people near his workspace. Ethan didn't care, but he felt unwelcomed. He noticed David's glare, with an eye-roll, toward Uncle Julian. Ethan assumed David forced their invitation to the house. Of course, from her glance toward David, Ethan figured his mother helped.

"How long y'all fixin' to stay?" Julian dropped the last bag in the room. At the same time, David side-eyed Uncle Julian, biting his lip as if holding back words.

"Until we have enough money," Kendra smiled. She dropped the smirk once Uncle Julian turned away.

The doorbell rang and Uncle Julian headed to the front. Before Julian could protest, a woman stepped through the door. Ethan noticed her baby bump as she tried to tuck her shirt over it. She used to have an hourglass frame but now had a bowl-shaped appearance.

He thought pregnancy was inevitable for his older cousin, Lanna. Her social media had photos of her drinking and twerking on shirtless guys. Nonetheless, he didn't judge, but she was a college girl. By all means, he admitted she had a wild side. Yet, the facade hid her insecurities— her flaws. Even now, she hunched over, smiling and hiding her stomach again. Despite this, Lanna's online persona was quite different. Her comment section mentioned her as untamed, free-spirited, and trendy. Yet, Ethan thought of her as the expectations and isolation that came with fame. To him, she was her own critic and paparazzi. Even when they were younger, her hair resembled a Mohawk, but she had a tamed voice.

Now, a few of Lanna's afro-curls got into Ethan's eye as she hugged him. It was a bear hug, if the animal was pregnant and smelt like lavender. She almost squeezed the life out of him, but oddly, he didn't mind. This was his older cousin after all. Lanna was one of the first people to check on him after the incident. Compared to his mother, Lanna was patient. A bit surprising from his cousin, the wildfire, but she showed a calm affection toward him. Back then, those couple of weeks were difficult, and he didn't leave his room, unless he had to pee. Even so, Lanna called and offered to take a flight to keep him company-- He refused. Of course, he appreciated the attempt, but he didn't want his cousin to visit to only watch him sulk. For the most part, she pushed harder for them to move to Mississippi than his mother.

"Welcome to the Sipp! Um, want me to show y'all 'round? Or, ya know, it's up to you. Whatever y'all wanna do." Lanna laughed, while appearing stiff.

"Uh, I don't know..." Ethan turned toward his mother, a bad move. His mother stared at him the way she did in the car. He knew her meddling ways, but he was helpless to do anything.

"Ethan would love that, correct?" His mother smiled which Ethan knew was a warning before she started to nag. It's something he hated.

Ethan nodded his head in obedience, well, more like in fear. Yet, it shouldn't be bad, right? His cousin mentioned they were going to drive around or go to a small store. In that case, there wouldn't be many people around.

Once outside the gates, Ethan followed her to an old pickup truck. When she pulled the handle, Lanna hopped into the car and started the engine. From the rumbling, the vehicle didn't sound safe. He admitted the thought of dashing inside, but *it* caught his attention.

Ethan jerked his head to something moving in the bushes. It was in the shrubs at the neighbor's house. Observing closer, it had a long snout and ears facing Ethan's direction. In the distance, the four-legged creature, mid-sized, with a bushy tail, appeared to stalk him.

After he focused his vision, Ethan realized he was staring at a fox. Ethan had an eerie feeling about the creature, something unnatural. Given that the fox had gray fur like a storm had made him feel uneasy. In particular, the type of storm to demolish homes. Then, its eyes, like hellish fire, seemed to study him. In fact, the fox's gaze seemed more like that of a serial killer than a mindless animal.

Ethan felt like the fox wanted to rip out his throat, but he fought the urge to run. Even though he doubted he would survive the escape. The same feeling made goosebumps sprint up his arm. It was as if someone rubbed a cold blade across his skin. Out of fear, Ethan jumped into the car and slammed the door. Lanna glanced at him, about to ask if the trip would be too soon, but she disregarded his jitteriness. Once they drove off, he felt the feeling fade. It dissipated as they got farther away from the house.

CHAPTER 2

The engine knocked as if a hammer slammed against rusted parts. Ethan tested the seat belt around his chest. It seemed sturdy, but he hoped it wouldn't trap him in a burning car. Ethan couldn't shake the image of a wreckage and limps scattered across the concrete.

Lanna's phone rang. Then, she raised it to eye level. A heavy sigh, almost a grunt, came out as she glanced at the caller ID. She answered. Her eyes rolled as if regretting to answer, but her voice, when she spoke, held a tone of familiarity. Annoyance. Ethan wondered if his mother was checking on them, another annoying tactic. Lanna's eyebrows formed harsh angles above flared nostrils. Yet, the soft tone of her voice picked words with care. She said, yes ma'am and no ma'am like she practiced this moment her entire life. Ethan couldn't understand the conversation from his side, but Lanna appeared irritated.

Lanna sighed. "We gotta swing by my place, if that's alright with you. I gotta pick someone up, and it won't take long, I promise."

"Okay?" Ethan watched as Lanna made a U-turn, almost hitting the curb.

The ride to Lanna's house let Ethan pass the rural area of Mississippi. The fields of wheatgrass under the blazing sun appeared burnt. Their tips whipped and lashed in the wind under a dim sky, cloudy enough to cast shadows on the concrete. Deeper into the south, the road shifted to cracked cement, and the road signs appeared dull and dead. In this area, things withered, brick buildings had shattered windows, and splintered doors. The neighborhood appeared deserted, a ghost town. There was no one else besides a man, in rags, digging in the trash. Ethan assumed the man was searching for scraps. From his wild bulging eyes, the man looked like an addict. Ethan watched as the man yanked a used needle from the garbage. The man, with his needle and a bag, disappeared into the woods as they drove away.

The car slowed as they approached a house. Compared to the other area of the neighborhood, it was in better condition. Yet, still an undesirable place. The grass was a shade of dirt while the naked trees were drained of life. The branches seemed exhausted.

Almost hunched toward the ground where the land had been beaten with whisky bottles. Shattered glass scattered across the drive-way where a truck had broken down. The vehicle had dents like a bruise and deep scratches. From under the truck, oil spilled down the driveway like blood. This dark liquid gathered near the mailbox. Floating in the oil was a dead Caroline Chickadee.

Lanna parked next to the mailbox with the word Hare. The family's last name was Hare, so this must've been Lanna's place. From the truck, Ethan jumped after hearing two people yelling. Onc was a male's voice, raspy as if strained lungs tried to produce sound. The other person, a female, had a strident voice. It reminded Ethan of a metal scratching across glass. The woman's cussing seemed to overpower the man.

"You a fuckin' junkie!", a strident but familiar voice yelled.

Ethan's stomach churned at the harsh voice echoing from around the garage. It took a moment for him to realize, but the voice was Aunt Chrystal. Her shouting carried around the neighborhood like a blaring horn. Her eyes feral and fixed on her target, slamming her hands together. Clapping on each syllable. Facing her was Uncle Ezekiel, known as Zek, his lips blackened like cigarette ash. He swatted at her comment, his face filled with disgust as if the words slapped him. His whining revealed that he didn't completely dodge the verbal blow.

"You a selfish bitch! Ya hear? I don't need no money... Mama needs it." Uncle Zek raised his chin.

"Mama ain't got no cash 'cause you a thief! How she gonna let a crackhead stay in the house, huh!? Everyone else gets kicked out, but the damn junkie. A FUCKIN' JUNKIE!" Aunt Chrystal inhales, "You know what…? Keep killin' yourself, but don't come askin' me for help!" Aunt Chrystal snorted.

"Don't ya care 'bout me? You my sista'!" Uncle Zek's last words came out brittle.

Aunt Chrystal snickered. "Sista'? If Pa didn't give a damn, why should I?"

Uncle Zek's eyes turned away from her. His chin and shoulders crumpled as if wounded. Restless nights became evident as the man drooped, holding his breath. His posture could've been from smoking, an induced fog. Most times, Uncle Zek's mind drifted into a haze, lost in his recreation. Ethan had seen him intoxicated, and at times, noticed his red eyes, but never like this. Aunt Chrystal's belittlement had inflicted pain. A deep sorrow his uncle seemed to hold in his chest but couldn't restrain. Uncle Zek stormed off in the other direction, gripping his shirt. Ethan thought he saw a tear slip from his uncle's face, but the man was gone before Ethan was certain.

Looking away from her phone, Lanna started beating the horn, several times. She seemed to search for Aunt Chrystal, unaware of Uncle Zek's absence. Ethan's aunt looked agitated as she stomped to the truck, but Lanna kept honking. His cousin didn't seem to care about her mother's anger. Her expression said— *they had things to do*. Ethan scooted over trying to avoid conflict with Aunt Chrystal as she slammed the door. Once situated in the truck, they took off to the store. A trail of smoke followed the old vehicle like a dark cloud.

#

"I need supplies from that new store", Chrystal demanded.

Lanna butted in. "I know you prefer that store, but not there. The other store is closer, and everything we need is there."

Aunt Chrystal frowned, until Lanna nodded toward Ethan, who was staring out the window. He watched as they passed cars and crowds of people, the new store his aunt had mentioned. Judging from the chaos of carts, he assumed they avoided the place because of him. Ethan admitted the place seemed busy— overstimulating. So, instead of the new store, Lanna pulled into "Pennies". The parking lot was small, and quiet, with few people. Indeed, this was where he needed to be. After turning into a spot, the three of them hopped out and entered the store.

Pennies was like any other low-priced business. The place had 50 cent paper towels, cheap candy, plastic cups, or anything affordable. Another great thing was no people, besides the employees working.

Ethan had felt nervous before but there didn't seem to be a reason to worry. Aunt Chrystal headed down the cleaning section. Then, Ethan and Lanna walked to the food aisle. In the frozen section, they found ice cream. More than he expected. The store had popsicles, sherbet, vanilla, strawberry, and the selection continued. The pregnant lady, Lanna, was digging through the treasure they had found. Yet, Ethan had felt a chill slither down his spine. The freezer was frosty, but it wasn't that type of chill.

He turned around to find a woman staring at them. She walked in their direction. Her uniform suggested she worked at the store. So, she could've been checking on them, but it made him feel uncomfortable. Ethan noticed the woman following them around the store, but he tried to ignore the feeling. From the end of the aisle, the woman's choppy hair made her look unhinged. Most likely a few screws were loose in her head. Also, the woman had a huge wart on her nose. The wrinkles on her face made her appear like a witch.

Lanna found the ice cream she wanted, and Ethan snatched something random. They started heading to the snack aisle while the hag stalked. Now in this aisle, the crone was closer from arm's length. If she wanted to grab Ethan she could, but instead she kept staring. Something felt wrong about the woman. From this distance, Ethan thought she was close enough to stab him. Lanna noticed Ethan's body tense and then looked over his shoulders. She found a lady glaring at them.

"Ya good?" Lanna stepped up.

"Y'all buyin' somethin'?" The crone hissed.

"Duh, we ain't stealing'."

The hag raised a brow. "Are ya? I don't trust you…people."

Lanna's lips twisted as if she ate something bitter. Almost Burnt. Agitated. Intense as Lanna's glare. Entitled should've slipped her mind. Obnoxious? No, the hag was ignorant. Yeah, that's the word she thought. He was sure. Ethan saw Lanna clinch her mouth. An expression that caused him to shrink back. Her fist trembled as her chest swelled, shrouding around fury, a repressed madness. Then, he covered his ears as she burst out, cursing the old crone.

Aunt Chrystal cut the corner as she saw Lanna screaming at the hag. His aunt stormed toward them, yanking up her baggy overalls. This was her fighting stance before she slammed someone's face into the snacks. Of course this wasn't the first time. Ethan remembered when someone pissed off his aunt. The person was tall, a heavy-set dude in his 20's or older. The big man disrespected her which ended with the guy's face in a bag of bloody chips.

Aunt Chrystal stomped. "What's goin' on?!"

Lanna explained the situation while Aunt Chrystal glanced at the old hag. Then she looked at Lanna as she spoke, and back at the hag again. Ethan wondered what was going through his aunt's head. Seeing that her eyes twitched, and her face turned a strange red, like hot metal. Aunt Chrystal looked like the blow horn that was about to explode. Then, Ethan saw the old crone smirk. Yet, it turned into fear once his aunt noticed. The old woman inched away as if regretting the decision. Even so, it was too late since his aunt was already cussing out the hag. Aunt Chrystal's yells attracted the other employees to the scene. Their heads peeked into the aisle as they observed three women arguing near the snacks. Even though his aunt's screaming alarmed the employees, it wasn't as menacing as her clenched fist. His aunt's hands flew in wild motions as she spoke. In response, the old woman's eyes, like a lizard, swelled. The wicked crone, with hair like serpents, started to inch back. Now, the woman resembled a trembling Chihuahua barking. In a last attempt to hold power, she pulled an object from her pocket.

"I'm callin' 9-1-1!" the jittery crone threatened. The woman dialed the numbers and started talking to the operator. She used words like thugs, thieves, and ghetto to describe them.

Aunt Chrystal began hurling items at the skittish woman, aiming at her face. Before Aunt Chrystal could try to flip the woman, red and blue lights flashed from outside. Ethan assumed someone called the cops before the old hag did. A policeman, with a fat face and a stubble beard, rushed over to the aisle. Then, the cop yanked his aunt from almost ripping out the crone's matted hair. While this ended a fight, it seemed to have started a new one since Aunt

Chrystal glared at the cop. In hopes to end police violence, Lanna stepped in, explaining their side of the story. Also, Aunt Chrystal added a few angry slurs.

The crone had tears falling down her cheeks which the cop seemed to notice. Ethan thought the crocodile tears could've swayed The Officer's verdict. Since, from a distance, he observed The Officer's hand on the gun holster. A ready firearm, but for who? For them, yes, he assumed but Ethan knew they weren't in the wrong. Of course, with her best effort, Lanna argued the case to the man in blue as well. Yet, this claim seemed irrelevant. Seeing as The Officer's grip tightened on the gun.

Then, Ethan stared at The Officer's face. The man's beard was a stubble of needles while his eyes were icy, an arctic blue. His fat face, like a goblin, was an oily ball of meat. Sweat dripped from The Officer's chin as Lanna reasoned with him. Under his jaw, a fox tattoo etched the flesh of his neck. A mark of intimidation and wickedness beneath the skin. Ethan noticed tension in the cop's body language. It was obvious the man stayed vigilant and never exposed his back. As The Officer's eyes darted between them, Ethan could feel a sense of unease. Ethan knew in this world, scared, or disturbed people kill, like the police, the hag, and his dad's killer. They were the ones who shouldn't hold a gun or wield power. Ethan glanced, with teary eyes, at The Officer. He hoped the police wouldn't shoot. Ethan didn't want to be another tragedy like his father. Standing in the aisle, his flashbacks started to gush out like an open wound. He held his breath, shutting his eyes as if suppressing the pain. Ethan wanted to hide in the dark, somewhere safe. Even though this moment had familiarity and a strange kinship, he didn't want the memories.

The hag pointed at his aunt, with weary fingers, which made Aunt Chrystal yell again. Ethan watched as The Officer unclipped his holster. Ethan felt as if the gun pointed at him. The barrel aiming at his body. Ethan clenched his shirt; it felt like someone had shot him, though he knew this wasn't true. Even so, his chest tightened up as if a bullet burnt through his flesh. His heart knocked against his chest like a broken engine. While his breathing was a sequence of irregular exhaling, and inhaling. After that, he exhaled longer, and then didn't breathe at all.

Ethan collapsed.

The world around him was darker. Even with blurred vision, he saw Lanna turn her head toward him. Her eyes displayed a type of terror that even made him scared. His cousin said something, but Ethan couldn't hear over himself gasping for air. Now, his eyes locked on The Officer's loaded gun.

"Put the gun away! It's makin' him panic."
Lanna trembled, rushing over to Ethan.

From behind her, The Officer tried to assist Ethan. Yet, the boy flinched. Then, the cop noticed his fingers on the pistol and withdrew his hand. The policeman backed away from Ethan as Lanna tried to calm the boy's nerves. Aunt Chrystal and the crone stood in silence as well. However, they weren't the only two watching. A crowd of employees formed around Ethan like a funeral service. They seemed to mourn or pity him. Ethan couldn't see much but could sense eyes on him. He felt them staring. Judging.

He knew he looked stupid.

Ethan gazed at the ceiling. He shouldn't have left the house. Yet, he listened to his mother. He should've ignored her. Protested at least. Instead, he laid on the floor, surrounded by strangers, in this store.

He wanted to hide again. Disappear.

He had a gut feeling this might happen. Ever since he saw that fox, Ethan had felt off, uneasy. In the corner of his blurred vision, he saw a bushy tail vanish into the crowd. The strangeness of it didn't seem to register in his panicked mind.

Lanna helped her cousin stand up. For Ethan's sake, without attitude, Aunt Chrystal finished explaining the situation to the cop. The Officer seemed to take mental notes and then gave the hag a warning. This almost caused Aunt Chrystal to flick off the man, but Lanna stopped her. Both of them stared at Ethan as he struggled to stand. After examining the back of his head, Lanna claimed she didn't see any blood or a lump. Ethan sighed with relief since he didn't like hospitals. Yet, they needed to get home, and he wanted to leave. The Officer asked if Ethan needed medical attention, but Lanna refused his offer.

While supporting him, she mumbled something under her breath, making Aunt Chrystal snicker. His aunt glanced at The Officer, but it seemed the cop didn't hear the insult. Lanna told The Officer her cousin was fine. Also, Ethan's mother couldn't afford medical bills. So, The Officer stepped back and let them go. While passing the cop, Lanna rolled her eyes as she guided Ethan to the exit. Ethan heard another mumble under her breath. He assumed Lanna wanted the lady arrested instead of given a warning. Whereas Aunt Chrystal wanted to kick the lady in the chest. Ethan didn't care, feeling exhausted from the incident. He assumed his aunt noticed his exhaustion; she huffed and swung away from him toward the crowd.

Aunt Chrystal started shoving the other employees out of their way. This helped them step out the front doors. Yet, before they left, the hag tried to apologize, but Aunt Chrystal flicked off the crone as they walked out. This made the knotted haired woman gasp. Somehow the crone seemed surprised by his aunt's gesture. They ignored the hag's tears as Lanna assisted Ethan into the car. At the same time, Aunt Chrystal spit on the parking lot and slammed the door. Then, they drove away.

CHAPTER 3

"Take me home", Chrystal demanded.

"Ethan first, then you. I'm not bein' rude, but please don't rush me. Okay? I'm tired and wanna get home safe. That's all." Lanna muttered.

Chrystal frowned, sinking into her seat as the rest of the ride fell into a silence.

Once they drove into the driveway, Ethan assumed Lanna called his mother and David. Seeing that they were already outside. Kendra shoved David, with eyes full of tears, as she guided her son out the car and into the house. David staggered behind her as they made their way to the bedroom.

Coming from the backyard, Uncle Julian and Uncle Zek were screaming. Uncle Zek, who must've snuck past the gate, invaded Uncle Julian's face. So close that the two were almost nose to nose.

"Back up!" Uncle Julian shoved him.

Uncle Zek stumbled but then shot up. He clenched his fist, stomping forward. Twitching. Uncle Julian ripped off his tie at that moment.

Before either of them could throw a punch, an old lady stepped between the two grown men. The small woman, with gray hair in a bun, yelled something at Zek and pointed to a car. Uncle Zek, pouting droopy black lips, unclenched his fist and headed to the car. The old lady with a cane, but sturdy, stepped around Julian without a word.

"You ain't welcome here" Julian grumbled.

"I'm here for mah grandbaby, not you. It won't take long." She entered the house.

Ascending the stairs with steady steps, Charlene, known as Mama, called for Kendra. Upon reaching the upstairs hallway, Kendra led Mama to one of the guest rooms. The old lady stepped in, finding her grandson staring at the ceiling. She gazed, not at him, but seemed to watch an old memory.

"It's like I'm seein' my boy in you, remindin' me of my pride and joy. As a mother, it's comfortin'." The old lady smiled, shifting her gaze to the window. She seemed lost in another flashback, or already bored with the interaction.

Ethan watched Granny as she eased herself onto the bed, rubbing her knees as she sunk into the mattress. The funeral was the last time he saw Granny Charlene. Similar to when she stared down at the casket, the old woman gazed at Ethan the same way. She must've felt as if she was losing her son again, his dad. However, his mother argued that Granny Charlene was at the funeral for attention. Better yet, his mother claimed that Granny was there for the fame she always wanted. His mother mentioned Granny didn't care about his dad, until he died. Ethan assumed his mother was jealous of the attention the crying old lady was receiving. During the funeral, his mother had spilled wine on Granny by accident, but Ethan didn't believe it was a mistake. For this reason, Granny Charlene had to leave early which his mother had planned.

Even now, as she stood by the door, he noticed his mother rolled her eyes. On the bed, Granny set her cane aside and laid a hand on his arm, her touch felt like wrinkled scales. Her grin appeared twisted as she glanced at him, discarding the smile once she released his arm. He wasn't sure if he liked that gesture but played along with the facade. She gave Ethan a squeeze, then sprung up from the bed.

Kendra smiled at Mama as the old lady took her cane and made her way out the room. Once Granny left, Kendra's smile dropped. It looked as if his mother ate something bitter, and he could relate.

On the bottom of the stairs, Uncle Julian watched the old lady with squinted eyes. She stepped down the stairs without haste.

Mama lifted her chin, with a flared nose as if she smelled something foul. "Hmm." Then, she walked toward the door.

In return, Julian raised a brow as she stepped out of the house. Mama couldn't dwell long, or rather she didn't want to stay. Then, Mama looked back at

Julian. She hated coming to this house. The old lady turned around and walked to the car.

Without hesitation, Julian slammed the door. Before Julian reached the stairs, banging echoed from the entrance. The man raised his brow again, ready for an old lady to smack him. However, Julian's raised brow was now an expression of bewilderment as Lanna rushed in. Julian was unable to protest since Lanna was already up the stairs.

Ethan's cousin found him lying in bed, bathed in a soft, warm light filtering through the curtains. From outside, a car horn signaled Aunt Chrystal's impatience. Lanna grunted, then hugged him with a softer touch before leaving the room. Ethan wished she could stay longer, but he understood dealing with a difficult mother.

David lingered, giving Kendra a reassuring smile before leading her downstairs. Now alone, Ethan became aware of the ticking of the clock on the wall. Each rhythmic beat seemed to echo in the room, creating a melody that soothed him. He sunk deeper into the pillow, his gaze fixed on the clock. Each passing minute felt like a gentle wave, washing away the events of the day, erasing every mistake. After a couple of ticks, he closed his eyes, letting the peacefulness of the moment wash over him.

#

Ethan stood in the middle of a mall, a huge, dead space. The place seemed quiet. Miserable. Everything motionless as if stuck in a phantom layer of ice. In the distance, Ethan noticed the light revealed dust trapped in mid-air. The particles, confined within the force, resembled frosted glass. In the haze, it imprisoned the people as well. Unlike Ethan, treading around the crowd, these prisoners were stuck in time. Such as the kid snared on the escalator. The boy was like the others. A hostage. Next to the child, Ethan noticed a small tree with holes in the leaves. It appeared insects had gnawed on its withered tips. The leaves, like the color of blood, drooped as if exhausted. In this frozen mall, the tree moved as if a breeze passed through. Whereas nothing else had budge.

Then, the haze from the sky turned into darkness. Trying to feel his way through the mall, Ethan felt something stalking him.

Ethan paused. He heard it. Rather he believed he did. Then, Ethan hesitated to step away. He couldn't see it, but something was moving around him. Then, a hanger dropped.

Ethan jerked his head to the darkest part of the mall, a clothing store. The atmosphere from this distance felt cold. Uninhabited. Stepping closer, he noticed the walls appeared sickly like grass in the winter. The floor tiles looked as if dirty snow was caught between grooves.

A slight movement in the shadows caught his attention.

At first, Ethan thought he was looking at a pile of jeans, but its silhouette shifted into a four-legged creature. The fox, with stormy fur, unveiled itself from the shadows. Predator-like eyes gazed at Ethan, approaching him with a lowered head as if on the hunt. The fox revealed its canine teeth but instead of a growl, the animal chuckled.

Ethan stepped back, stumbling, almost falling. He caught himself and then stared at the fox. From its bushy tail and pointed ears, he thought it was a fox.

Yet, this creature cackled, not like a hyena, but as if a man with a raspy voice. More like a hardy, sickened sound. Its eyes, glowing in the dark like a torch, turned to the back of the store. The fox sprinted and disappeared into the clothes rack. Ethan felt the creature retreated from some unseen force, a threat he couldn't put into words.

The muted sound of a bell chimed as if underwater. The haunting shrill, like the wrong music note, moved through the frozen world. And Ethan felt something coming.

His eyes dashed around to find an exit. Something red, an arrow, any sign of a door, but nothing. He needed to escape. It didn't matter how, but it had to be now. If only he could see a door.

Ethan looked around. The crowd of people blocked his view. Then, he yelled at a girl to move.

Silence.

He turned to a man and yelled to run.

Cold. Silence.

Of course that wouldn't work. They're trapped like Ethan. Oh shit, he was stuck like them.

Ethan almost shoved the woman next to him, but an eerie sensation paralyzed his body.

A pitch-black figure emerged from the shadows, taking shape as it floated into view. The figure's outline suggested a worn straw hat, yet it merged into the darkness, making it hard to discern. Even as he stared at the entity, its form slipped from his gaze. It appeared distorted and twisted like unclean smoke.

The creature's neck leaned as if broken and its limbs turned in the wrong direction. Although the creature was a few feet away, he couldn't understand the thing's physics.

It appeared as 2D but moved in 3D space. The thing twitched, viciously, like a glitch on a screen. Its eyes, similar to the color of a serpent, flared up as it inched closer to him. However, Ethan couldn't move.

Tears fell from his eyes as he tried to fidget. He wanted to move something. Anything. He could start from his toes and then work his way to his legs. Ethan tried but his toes didn't budge. Not even an inch. Wait, he could try his fingers up to his arms, right? No, that didn't help either. It seemed His fingers surrendered. More like his body submitted to the creature. Which made more tears fall from his face.

Ethan stared at the creature, feeling an icy chill engulf him, numbing his senses. Its disfigured claws and silhouette embodied death, a being that had never lived. A gasp escaped Ethan's lips as he struggled to breathe, as if the air around him had thickened like blood. He felt a pull, as though dragged into a dark void, his head spinning, stomach churning. Fighting to stay conscious, he grappled with his own identity. What was his name again? Ah, yes... E-Ethan, Ethan Hare.

He seemed to regain consciousness as he stared into a pit of anger and a darkness he couldn't understand. Ethan watched as the thing's crooked arm reached out. What appeared to be its hand, gripped a familiar object. It pointed the object at Ethan. Then, a loud bang erupted from the end of it.

Ethan woke up.

CHAPTER 4

Bang!

The truck swerved. The hissing didn't seem to come from the engine but rather something else.

Lanna sighed. She assumed they hit a pothole.

She turned the wheel to pull over the car. Lanna, 12-weeks pregnant, crouched to the ground. She held onto her dress which didn't touch the dirt. Then, she brushed the curls from her face and examined the flat tire. Lanna grumbled. She realized the spare was already in. It had been used last week since the town neglected to fix the potholes, and she hadn't had time to buy a new one.

From under the truck, Lanna watched as her mother's heels hit the ground. Then, the crunching sound made its way to the other side of the car. The thudding paused. Her mom, Chrystal, twisted her lips. Lanna assumed her mom disliked seeing her pregnant daughter trying to repair a tire.

Lanna glanced at her mom. The woman had baggy overalls and heels, instead of her usual combat boots. Chrystal looked like a southern woman. Rather than flowers and sweet tea, think of thorny roses that smelled like moonshine and WD-40. She bathed, but today her clothes were free of oil stains. She worked with cars unlike most ladies around town who were concerned with the southern belle aesthetic. Such as cute sundresses and straw hats. Whereas her mother preferred muscle, shouting, and a fight. Rather than lipstick, mumbled words and submission. Lanna's mother always said there wasn't time to be polite when a shotgun could stop a man from taking what he wanted. Her mom could fix the truck, better than she could, but only if Lanna hadn't forgotten to buy a spare.

Lanna kicked the stupid tire. Then, she glanced at her mom. *I told you so*, her mother might've thought. Another reason to call her daughter irresponsible. Or childish. Or a dumb tramp.

Lanna hit the tire again.

She glanced as her mom grunted. Then, Chrystal headed to the trunk and removed a bag.

"Where's the spare?" Chrystal took the tools out of the bag.

"Don't have a spare…"

"Great…" Chrystal threw the lug wrench in the bag.

Lanna noticed her mother's mouth tense up like a lion's jaw. Which was nothing new. She turned away from the tempered woman and stared at the spare.

She forgot to buy a tire. Like, really?! This wasn't Lanna who had never made mistakes. It's obvious her social media accounts contained photos with great quality. The light always glistened on her bronze skin; at just the correct angle. The camera needed to capture her flawless curves. She required perfection because one bad pose would cause people to unfollow her. She couldn't risk the tiniest fault. Lanna's actions affected her reputation online but also in town.

Her followers called her the angel with a golden smile. Yet, people in town claimed she acted like her wrathful mother. Sometimes she hated those comments. Although Lanna knew how to do things herself, like her mom. Then again, she still despised the comparison.

Lanna knew how to trim the sides of her head and line up the edges as if a professional barber. Some referred to her as the prettiest mechanic or the gorgeous chief. She could do it all. Even when she practiced a new skill, she never posted her mistakes. It wasn't as if Lanna hid under concealer, like Aunt Kendra, or boasted her gut like her mother. In either case, she wanted everyone to believe they could depend on her, and most people trusted beautiful women. No pain in high heels or no crying while helping her mother make extra money. As a child, if Lanna wanted a Christmas gift, she had to work for it. That meant she had to be productive. She needed to make something of herself. After all, Lanna hated dealing with avoidable flaws.

If she hadn't been distracted from last week's drama, then they wouldn't have been in this situation. Now, two miles of nature's abyss stood between them and the nearest auto shop. She walked around examining the overgrown maze that stretched several acres. The road itself vanished into the labyrinth of the void. In this area, most of the street lights didn't work. Which was the only beacon of civilization in sight.

Lanna paused. In fact, this road didn't have any lights at all. She jolted around, then turned again. She only saw the veil of trees and a forgotten road.

Lanna glanced at her phone. Yup, no service. She tossed it. Shit! She threw her phone! Lanna ran to pick it up. She pressed the power button and the screen lit up. Good, it didn't break.

Lanna sighed as she saw no signal.

Then, she noticed her mom trying to push the truck. It didn't budge. Of course, but her mom kept shoving from the back.

From the look of the sky, it would be pitch-black in an hour. Lanna, already ensnared by the shadows of the trees, could only imagine the things that lurked in the night.

Lanna jumped.

Someone from behind honked at them. Lanna noticed a tow truck slowing down, stopping behind their vehicle. A chunky man with a lemon peppered beard, maybe in his 40's, had hopped out.

"Need help?" the tow truck man asked.

"We're good, bye." Chrystal gestured to Lanna to come over. Knowing her mother, the woman wanted to push the car to the shop. Whereas Lanna didn't want to dirty herself.

"Ah, that'd be a godsend! If ya don't mind?" Lanna walked over to the man.

Lanna didn't plan to be out in the dark. She heard of women dragged into shadows, enduring unspeakable horrors. On the news, they found bodies in the morning with insects gnawing on dead flesh. There wasn't a guarantee the tow truck man wasn't planning to kidnap them, or enslave them into sex trafficking. However, the known was better than the unknown.

Lanna shifted her gaze from the man and glanced at their truck. She kept a gun in the vehicle, a source of confidence, but she forgot it at home. Lanna bit her lip, turning her face from the man's gaze. She hoped he didn't sense her fear. The tow guy could exploit their vulnerability due to her carelessness. Regardless of the fact, they needed a ride. The tow truck man could drive them to the auto shop. Unless he had sinister intentions. Whereas it was impossible to know what was hiding in the dark. To be honest Lanna felt something staring at them now.

Lanna turned around but only saw the branches sway. She swore something else moved but it could've been the shadows shifting from the dying sun.

From a distance, Lanna's mom crossed her arms. Chrystal glanced from Lanna to the tow guy. Then she huffed, turning her head away.

"You a psycho?" Chrystal's gaze drifted into the woods. Her eyes narrowed as the shadows gathered around them.

"Naw, I saw two ladies stranded on the road. Yo' car broke down, right?"

Chrystal jerked her head around. "You think we're helpless?!"

The tow guy glanced at Lanna and then back at Chrystal. "Uh, naw. I can tow yo' truck. Unless y'all planned on pushin' it in the dark? And isn't she pregnant?" The tow guy pointed at Lanna.

Her mother fell into a hush. An unsettling stillness for a woman whose voice erupted the room. Now audible, a whisper of the wind floated through the trees. The branches seemed to shiver with an anxiousness as if the forest waited for a response. Then, a grunt broke the quietness. Chrystal snatched the tool bag and headed to the tow truck.

"Thank ya kindly. I surely hope ya know we 'preciate your kindness." Lanna smiled at the man.

The tow guy tried to help her mom into his truck, but the woman stormed around, almost shoving him. After her mother stomped into the truck, Lanna noticed the bushes moving.

Lanna thought she saw something with gray fur. She examined the shrubs trying to see what was stalking them, but the man called over to her.

Lanna turned and saw their car loaded onto the tow truck. She glanced at the woods, but it was gone. She must've imagined it.

Lanna jumped into the truck and the man started the engine. Once the tow guy drove off, she released a breath of air. They were finally safe. Lanna glanced at their driver. Even though she didn't know the tow guy, she felt at peace with him rather than whatever lurked in the forest.

Lanna looked in the rear view mirror. From this distance, she could only make out a four-legged animal. Which shouldn't have seemed bizarre, but its gray fur spiked like a provoked feline. This suggested a hint of something more menacing beneath its facade. This could've been why something felt strange about the thing. She couldn't explain, but the creature made her stomach twist. At that moment, it lingered, as an ominous silhouette staring at them. A murderous intent seemed to cast from the creature like a killer's shadow. Yet, none of it mattered. They were off the road, and they were leaving the thing behind.

Lanna took a deep breath and then exhaled. She smiled. Yes, they were off the road.

As the bell jingled, Lanna and her mother stepped into the auto-shop. The lobby was a bit cramped but quiet with a scent of motor oil. On the other side, in the workshop, there were clamoring drills and flying sparks. Back in the lobby, Lanna walked over to the counter where a man, in a red uniform, was on the phone. As he talked, the man spoke with a simmering hushed tone. He gripped the cord, almost ripping it from the wall. After a couple of minutes, the man noticed Lanna and Chrystal. Then, he slammed the phone on the holder. He forced the corner of his lips to rise. Lanna assumed this was supposed to be a smile.

She explained the situation to the man, who then gave a price for the new tire. A good deal, but the wait was about an hour. Lanna handed the man the keys while her mom crossed her arms staring at the clock. Her mother appeared to glare as she watched the seconds tick.

The man walked into the workshop. As the door closed behind him, Lanna and Chrystal sat in the waiting area. Across from them was an older man, around her grandmother's age, texting. The old man was wearing a graphic t-shirt with a cartoon character and ripped jeans. Lanna thought he almost looked like a skateboarder. She wondered if his grandkids convinced him to wear that. Something for the kids to post online. Then, the old skater noticed Lanna gazing at him. The old man gave a slight wave and a smile. Chrystal noticed the man waving at her daughter.

"Whatcha lookin' at!?" Chrystal shot up from her seat.

The older man, startled, went back to texting. Lanna rolled her eyes. She disliked her mother's rudeness, a fury extending to everyone. If not for Lanna, her mother would've pushed the vehicle for miles instead of letting the tow truck guy help. While coupled with her mother yelling at the old man without any logic she could understand. Lanna often depended on her own resources, but her mother took self-reliance to the extreme. There were even times Lanna wasn't allowed to assist her. Days like these brought flashbacks from her childhood by the Mississippi River. While walking on the sand, her mother unleashed her rage on strangers, especially on men. All hell broke loose once a man had walked too close.

Before the outburst, her mother's grip seemed to hint at hidden tension. Even now, Lanna struggled to comprehend why that gesture left her feeling heartbroken.

"Why ya gotta be rude to him?" Lanna asked, watching as her mother appeared as if told not to breathe anymore.

"Why ya fixin' to git rid of it? Ya betta keep it than havin' an orphanage raise the child."

Lanna grumbled.

This woman just couldn't quit. This was the tenth time her mother asked, not expecting a change but desperately hoping. Well, Lanna had no intention of altering her decision. It's bad enough that she was too far along in her pregnancy. Even now, she wondered how she could be so stupid. Sometimes, Lanna thought about shoving pills down her throat, hoping to avoid childbirth. Then again, she might kill herself in the process. Her mother, having Lanna at a younger age, should've grasped the hardships of parenthood. Yet, her mother thought if she had to raise a kid then Lanna should too– that's the root of the problem. These conversations achieved nothing, leaving mother and daughter in a deadlock.

The constant guilt reflected in the test she failed last week. Lanna at her desk, half-awake, because the stress consumed her that night. She could ask for extra credit from the professor, but at this rate, Lanna wasn't graduating. Along with motherhood, she pondered if love blinded her judgment. While in class she thought of this decision she regretted. She imagined that she knew him, and almost believed in him. Lanna wanted to trust his love for her, but the messages on his phone read differently. Lanna had scrolled through the photos— with no underwear, revealing skin, and intimate pleasures. In response, he replied with heart eyes or a snap of the product between his thighs. Lanna compared him to a salesman because somehow, he sold her a lie. She felt stupid, to trust a delusion that envisioned him as a worthy dad. A complete and utter idiot that couldn't even read. Ever since she confessed about the pregnancy, he had blocked her calls— of course he did since he never loved her. Lanna dwelled on the ache, her mind drifting to the conversation at the restaurant. His hand recoiled at the news of impending fatherhood, leaving her alone at the table. Even now, the feeling had been suffocating her heart, fracturing whatever remained of herself. Since last week, a silent numbness, a weight of isolation had crushed her.

Chrystal took her daughter's hand. "We did a'right. Yo' granny done kicked us out, but we made it work. When that baby comes, I ain't gonna do that— I swear."

Again, Lanna sensed the secret tension in her mother's grasp. "I dunno…"

Keys jingled as the guy in the red uniform entered the lobby. He exchanged the car keys with Lanna while Chrystal swiped her card at the counter. Then, they stepped out of the shop. The old pick-up truck, now with a new tire, was parked in the front. In the parking lot, the two women shared a gaze. A subtle resentment that simmered beneath the surface of silence. A quietness that lasted from the walk to the car, lingering throughout the ride homeward.

CHAPTER 5

Ethan felt dizzy in bed, as if hit on the head. Once the haze cleared, he gazed into the mirror. He noticed his skin was a draining brown, as if he had seen a ghost flickering in the room. Yet, the entity was none other than himself. A teen with pimples, not nerdy, but burdened by school status because of his reservedness. Before him, the mirror unveiled teary eyes. The whites reddened from sleep or the weed from earlier. He needed substances, a distraction, to keep him sane. His fingers exposed a nervous tic, nail biting. Then, the sweaty stains gave evidence of a nightmare. At times, he sweated when meeting new people. He'd stare at the person without saying anything as if a hare in headlights.

After waking, the nightmare felt vivid, as if the shadowy figure floated nearby. In the dream, the fox from next door was present. He rarely dreamt about animals, and if he did, they never had humanoid speech. Ethan shivered; the nightmare's echo lingered in his mind. In fact, a similar night terror had followed his father's death. The mall and people were the same, except for the human statues. Also, the dark atmosphere with the black figure was absent from the other dream and the real event. Ethan shook the image from his head, avoiding conjuring the creature. Ethan could imagine its contorted body squirming in the corner of his room. He shifted his gaze, trying to stop thinking about it. Then Ethan heard laughing, drunken giggles, from down-stairs as he walked out of the room. He figured his mom, Uncle Julian, and David were having cocktails.

Ethan stepped off the bottom step of the staircase and then turned left into the living room. His mom and David were dancing while Uncle Julian sat sipping a glass of water. He noticed his mother allowed her bun to loosen, seeming to release the worry of debt. Ethan smiled, realizing she appeared happy, not what she displayed to others, but pure joy. In the cozy abode, his uncle wore a collared shirt instead of a suit. David stumbled, almost spilling his drink on the carpet. A maneuver Uncle Julian seemed to notice. He raised an eyebrow at David as if daring him to ruin the expensive material. Ethan sighed, a mix of gratitude for his mother's comfort but an unease that awaited David's slip up. David kept singing along with his mother, oblivious to Uncle Julian's warning. Of course, the two drunks didn't even notice Ethan walking into the room.

His mother noticed him first, holding up a drink with a steady hand. "Hey sweetie, want a margarita...virgin...?"

Ethan thought– *No, you drunken idiot*– but kept the comment to himself. Rather he said he was fine with water. He took the cup from her, evading her hands instead of pulled into her dance. Ethan settled beside his uncle, a heavy sigh escaping his lips. He watched as his mother stumbled, trying to gesture him to join her. A sting of regret set in as he glanced across the room. What was once his mother's relief now discomforted his chair. David laughed with his mother then headed to the bar. Another round to descend into slurred words and arguable decisions. Once everyone sat, David began telling them about the neighborhood.

David claimed they lived in a nice area. The neighborhood was a gated community with fancy parks and diving pools. Sometimes the neighbors were okay, if gossip wasn't spreading. David whispered that no one knew who engaged in the illicit activities. He suspected the neighbor next door delved in the black-market. Ethan wondered if that's why they had cameras, which made sense but would keep him up at night. David continued saying including the neighbor, some of their neighbor's income didn't add up. Whereas it could have been simple gossip.

David laughed at this as if telling a folktale. Uncle Julian added that storytelling was another way for the wealthy to pass time. His uncle said most of the residents, like himself and David, had an impressive income. However, they were white and middle-aged from the civil rights era. Meaning they weren't welcoming to everyone. His uncle said he knew David and himself weren't invited to certain events. Ethan detected an absence of concern in his uncle's words, but rather a subtle feeling of relief. Without another word, Uncle Julian resumed his reading. While David swigged his drink, each gulp seemed to feel like a bitter pill. David changed the topic.

Then, his mother asked how they kept the house clean. Ethan with a sigh had rolled his eyes, knowing she would ask that– again. David mentioned they had a maid named Ayo, who cleaned two or three times a week. David radiated, eager for Ethan and Kendra to see her tomorrow. Uncle Julian's grunt suggested that he and the maid didn't get along. Whereas David applauded her, saying how she was a big help with their gambling events. David and Uncle Julian would host parties, once or twice a week for the neighbors. Although Uncle Julian noted they limited the gatherings. His uncle mentioned an incident when someone directed a derogatory slur towards him. Uncle Julian claimed that people were in a fistfight and that the lawsuit was still ongoing.

Ethan peered out the window, wondering if the neighborhood was actually safe. David continued to speak, determined to dismiss Uncle Julian's comment. David's words sliced the air, with an edge of irritation. Although not because of Uncle Julian—there was something else bothering him. Ethan pondered whether David accepted the harsh reality. A possibility that the neighbors harbored a hate towards them. David tried to convince Ethan and Kendra that the neighborhood wasn't bigoted, racist. Yet, like his uncle, Ethan disagreed. Though his mother listened, searching for a beautiful yard and a perfect home. Something far from their flawed old house and ugly memories. David continued mentioning how they discussed business with drinks. The rich would boast about the newest charity they invested in. Ethan grinned, figuring it was an act of kindness to uplift the rich's ego.

David said something else, but the man's voice faded into a hum. Ethan heard the fox's raspy chuckle, but as his eyes darted around, no one else seemed to notice. An image clawed at Ethan's mind– a haunting black figure that seemed difficult to shake off. In his daze, he noticed the worry lines on his mother's forehead as if asking if he was okay. Ethan wanted to say yes but only managed to move the corner of his mouth. He needed to say something. Yet, he didn't want to talk about the fox and the dream. His mother already worried about him too much and the nightmare might cause her to freak out. He paused, the weight of unspoken thoughts hanging in the air. The seconds stretched into a prolonged silence. It imitated the struggle in Ethan's mind. He fiddled with the cup in his hand. His gaze lingered on the glass, searching for the right words.

"It's nothing. I'm sleepy." Ethan forced a yawn.

His mother didn't look convinced. She whispered, "It's about your father? About the…?"

"No!"

David stopped talking. Uncle Julian raised a brow and stared at his nephew gazing at the floor. Ethan sensed his family observing his behavior. In situations like this, he didn't know what to do but to avoid their gaze. They wanted the truth, but Ethan couldn't tell them about the dream. The family already thought the incident might have made him lose his mind. After the news got out about the therapy sessions, everyone looked at him as if he wore a straitjacket. He wished his mother hadn't said anything but was more annoyed that she couldn't leave things alone.

"You sure…?"

"Yes." Ethan sighed, still looking down.

His mother didn't seem to believe this comment either. Ethan could tell by the way she wiped the lipstick off her glass, trying to fix it. Getting up and walking to the kitchen's entrance, she gestured for him to follow her. He had to obey. He didn't want to, but at least she wasn't going to nag in front of Uncle Julian and David.

Ethan and his mother stepped into the kitchen. She sat at a stool and pulled one out for him. He sat waiting for his mother to rip the truth from his mouth but instead she stared at him. Either she was deciding what to say or this lecture was about a different incident. He admitted, this private discussion became unsettling.

"How are the online sessions? They're different than in person." His mother leaned toward him.

"They're okay." Ethan wanted this conversation to be over.

His mother paused. Either she waited for something, or for a different response. As he struggled to find words, Ethan observed her hair tied up in a bun. To those unfamiliar with Kendra, assumed this was a fashion. In reality, it had become a necessity, because she didn't have time for any other style. Like his mother's smile, the hair style, he assumed, kept people from asking if she was okay.

A brush of foundation concealed the dark circles under her eyes that came from sobbing. She had spent days and nights in the bathroom which she excused as *spa time*. This meant the shower drowned her tears. Despite her efforts, Ethan knew the truth--

her husband's death made her mascara bleed. Yet, she was *fine*; at least that's what she told Ethan.

He knew she clung to dad's worn-out jacket from college days. With the smell of her husband's jacket, she could control the width of her smile but not the laws of nature. In her mind, it seemed natural to manage her son rather than confronting her own issues. The constant barrage of worries began to weigh on Ethan more than his father's death.

He wished his mother would stop fighting so hard. Like a wounded patient, the only treatment was time. If possible, dull the pain until it felt bearable, not shoving down a cure like his mother. Staying positive couldn't resurrect the dead; such losses were irreversible. While he still missed his dad, wanted to heal from the event, it wasn't the same way his mother thought he should.

A miracle wasn't going to happen. Death, a concept that never crossed his mind, had struck Ethan. The permeance weighed heavy, gripping his mind. Uncertain about whether he could absorb the burden of the end. Again, he pondered how the day should've been different. He expected to buy new shoes and eat pretzels with pepperoni. Though a twist of fate revealed the events of that day. Everything happened in an instant. As chaos unfolded, his nerves screamed with dread. Now his mind, yelling at his muscles to unlock, rendering him paralyzed by the sight of a running crowd. His dad, the brave one, saved his life. Yet, the man who raised and loved him had bled out to death. Somehow Ethan could still face his family, despite being a coward. He believed the therapist might judge him, and his mother would hate her son if she knew. His mother took a towel and started wiping down a stain she couldn't clean. Ethan wished she would stop.

Kendra looked up at him. "You sure…?"

"S-Stop! You're… suffocating."

Kendra shot up. "Why haven't you opened up to me? Huh…!? Are you angry at me? Ashamed?" Kendra paused— then sighed, "Sometimes, it's as if you would've been better off with him than me."

"Maybe…" Ethan turned away from her. He waited for yelling but heard silence.

When he turned around, her stool was empty. He shouldn't have said that. What was wrong with him? Only a jerk would say something like that to his own mother. She would have drunk too much to remember, but he doubted it. Ethan huffed. This was hopeless.

Uncle Julian walked over to the cabinet and grabbed a glass. Then he started pouring water from the fridge. He took the empty seat, where Ethan's mother had been sitting, and drinking.

Uncle Julian scanned the room and leaned in saying, "Yo' mama needs to relax. I seen her wipin' down that fireplace in the other room."

Ethan laughed but only for a minute. He assumed Uncle Julian didn't know half of it. After laughing, they sat in silence for a moment. Then, Uncle Julian sat up, announcing his withdrawal to his office. His uncle claimed to have important business to take care of. The man also said that he didn't want to be around David and Kendra anymore. Feeling exhausted himself, Ethan followed his uncle. As they walked up the stairs, Ethan noticed there weren't any family photos on the walls. A question he had been meaning to ask since they came to him.

"Why do you live far away from the rest of the family?" Ethan asked.

Julian raised a brow, an unspoken thought behind his gaze. "Long story short: blood ain't always kinfolk."

He wondered what Uncle Julian meant. Then, Ethan thought about his time in Mississippi, at this house with the family. It did seem like everyone bickered. From his aunt and uncles arguing in the yard to Granny and his mother's death stare. Though it didn't seem like a legit reason for his uncle to hate the family. Siblings always didn't get along with each other, Ethan assumed since he was an only child. Also, sometimes mothers-in-laws and daughters-in-laws had conflicts. Well, that's what his mother said but he knew how she stretched the truth. Now thinking about it, his uncle could've been right. Even so, every time Ethan saw Granny, she would hug and kiss him. She rarely raised her voice, but his uncle might've experienced another side of her. Then Lanna seemed to dislike Granny as well. On the phone, his cousin mentioned Aunt Chrystal had blamed Granny for something. Lanna overheard the words— *it's your fault*. Ethan asked what she meant but Lanna claimed she didn't know. Whatever it was, it must've been horrible. He pushed the conversation to the back of his mind. As they stepped into the hallway, Ethan thought Uncle Julian mumbled *I didn't need the family*. However, Ethan was too tired to ask what his uncle meant. Uncle Julian went into his office then locked the door while Ethan headed back to his room. Ethan might ask about Granny later.

CHAPTER 6

In the living room, David stood behind the bar, the hum of a melody escaping his lips as he cleaned. In the quiet rest of the ensemble, he saw his reflection on the cocktail mixer. Today, as usual, David painted himself in earth hues. The colors pranced like the sunflower design on his collared shirt. Paired with shorts, and sandals, he dressed for the weather, equipped for the day's trip. He hoped Kendra, now his best friend, and Ethan would find comfort in the journey. No other reason came to mind for denying the simple pleasure of his plans. Reflecting on past interactions, David recalled people enjoying his thoughtfulness. Amongst colleagues, David was like honey-- a sweetness that extended beyond his politeness. They swarmed around David, drawn by his humor in the break room, where he lifted spirits. This might've been the reason that Julian held him close, finding relief in David's presence. Yet, in their intimacy, Julian said he discerned a naivety in David.

While wiping another glass, David rolled his eyes, recalling Julian's expression. A time when a con-artist scammed David. He remembered Julian's usual raised brow, scolding him for trusting in false words. At first, David admitted the deal seemed too good to be true. Yet, a question lingered-- why would a fellow bartender lie about wine? To his eyes, the bottle had the correct label and shape, a convincing facade. Now thinking about it, a sense of admiration dawned upon him, respecting the fine work. However, Julian questioned the bottle's authenticity and its distasteful hue. A week later, the truth came out about a man scamming people with counterfeit wine. The news reported the scammer took old bottles and filled them with grape juice to sell at a premium price. This information left David feeling disappointed. Although this sentiment fell short of the fury ignited within Julian. David understood Julian's wrath but also glimpsed behind the scammer's motives, a desperation. Despite residing in the comfort of his rich home, David grasped the harshness of life beyond the gate. Whenever he expressed this, Julian would stare in silence. He would compare his eyes to those of puppies and shake his head as an acknowledgement. David should've felt upset, but he accepted the compliment.

Julian also said his wavy hair appeared like a gentle ripple in a pond while his beard was like a wild bush. These comments reached to other aspects of his life. Like out in the grass, he did yoga to keep in shape. In fact, David wanted to run on this sunny day, but it was a rest day for everyone, especially Julian's nephew.

After cleaning the mini bar, David walked to the hallway entrance to meet Kendra. Then, he noticed Ethan coming down the stairs. The young man either had heavy eyelids from sleep or inhaling his herbs. David suspected the smoking scenario, due to the skunk smell drifting down the stairs.

Meanwhile, downstairs, David and Kendra waited. Despite the nephew's concerned face, today's purpose was a simple drive. Hearing that Kendra thought her son felt depressed, he figured the remedy might be fresh air.

Glancing at Kendra, he saw her bouncing on her toes, a contrast to her exhaustion yesterday.

Yesterday evening, the nephew's gaze and wide eyes hinted at an underlying distress. David sensed an unease that haunted beneath the surface. An emotion David couldn't grasp, yet an unspoken understanding lingered. From what Kendra told him, her husband's death casted a shadow on Ethan. Even Julian, eyes torn from his book, noticed an unrest on the nephew's face. David recalled Kendra gesturing Ethan into the kitchen to talk. Afterwards, like from their arrival, Kendra did her ritual. This time David observed her cleaning the fireplace. A subtle tension formed on Julian's brow, as he stared at his sister-in-law scrubbing. In his reading chair, Julian gripped the book while a whispering irritation raised. Without a word, David motioned him toward the kitchen, to console the nephew. Once Julian left, David approached Kendra, asking if she was okay. She claimed she needed rest since she drank too much. Yet, he suspected the cocktails didn't result in her teary eyes. Something else had happened in the kitchen. Besides bothering her, he gave his best friend some time alone.

Today, with clear eyes, she wore a flower-patterned shirt with shorts. It seemed she applied a lighter layer of makeup today, revealing bags under her eyes. He wondered if that was by choice or if she was saving her energy for later. He assumed she felt excited to explore the city as well.

"Ready...?" With skin hugging her eyes, Kendra smiled, showing a row of pearly white teeth.

David observed as the young man crossed his arms and narrowed his eyes toward his mother. At that moment, Ethan paused, scanning between him and Kendra. The nephew had a vigilant gaze related to Julian's, a stare that held suspicion for people. In this observation, David affirmed the kinship within the Hare's bloodline.

Despite the family nature of the trip, Julian wasn't joining them. Yet, the grumpy man, busy with work, agreed to cook dinner. Of course, Julian's way of apologizing for ditching them. It didn't matter; he prepared a delightful drive around town for Ethan and Kendra. David was about to enchant them with the wonders of Mississippi. As he jingled the car keys, he pranced on his toes like Kendra. Skipping out the house, he led her and Ethan to a blue SUV with white rims. It wasn't expensive like Julian's sports car, but David preferred comfort rather than luxury. Kendra took the front seat; Ethan stayed in the back, with noise-resistant headphones. Ethan moaned, scrolling through his phone while she shimmed to the radio. Then, David started the engine and drove off.

As they approached, a cluster of skyscrapers emerged on the horizon. The city sky had a morning hue with drifting noon clouds. Yet, toward the south of them, the country had a blazing sun with scarce clouds. Back in the city, the trees kept their old roots, like the rural areas, as the wind swept the dust. The breeze carried the unpleasant remnants of the Jim Crow laws. Despite this history, Kendra nudged him, waving at the residents in the summer street. Some of the pedestrians gave a brief wave, turning to bask in the sun. Unlike David's dancing eyes, their expressions seemed indifferent. David smiled, tapping the steering wheel on a rhythm, savoring the fleeting interaction.

The truck came to a halt at the redlight. Beside it, hooves on concrete echoed until the horse rider stopped. The man glanced over to their truck, tipping his cowboy hat in a friendly gesture. Kendra and David imitated the same greeting, giggled, and then the light shifted to green. They waved goodbye as the cowboy turned the corner, galloping away.

On the next corner, a lady with a cart juggled between filling cups of fruit and money. Beneath her straw hat, she sweated, rubbing her palms on her overalls before handing someone a cup. Judging by the line, it appeared everyone had a craving for fresh fruit. By the time one customer left, another had stepped up.

David, having driven past the fruit lady, continued his tour. They passed a civil rights museum, housing historic artifacts. The exhibits glorified the confederate south, entwined with African-American culture.

As he turned, the aroma of the black south embraced his senses. Such as the scent of fried chicken and collard greens that wafted from a nearby restaurant. The diner's parking lot overflowed with a bustling crowd of cars.

Beyond the restaurant, he drove past a flock of elderly ladies. The group wore sundresses and grand hats, waltzing along. In the southern sun, the women resembled a congregation of turkeys.

In the car, David told Kendra and Ethan about all the fun places to visit. Also, he mentioned things people frowned upon. They drove past some people talking and hugging on the street. One woman, with a fox coat, seemed friendly, offering more than hugs and kisses.

On a corner, a man sold medicine for those who needed it. Behind the man stood his friends, a crew of men in matching outfits. They hid protection under their shirts, watching out for the men in blue. David didn't care too much since everyone had to survive.

Instead of walking the streets, David suggested they go to the mall— or well, the mini zoo, and if possible, an empty park. Haunted by yesterday's incident, David sensed Kendra's hesitation about taking Ethan out. When Kendra answered Lanna's call that day, her lively demeanor had wilted. Her shoulders slumped, burdened by the weight of the conversation. Knees buckling, as if the words from the other end had drained the life from her being. When Ethan returned, Kendra and he had ushered the boy into the house. Ignorant of Ethan's state, David still discerned the emptiness in his gaze. A sorrow that echoed from the shadows of that past day. David remembered Kendra supporting Ethan up the stairs. Each step revealed the burden of his mental exhaustion.

David couldn't recall how Julian's brother died, but Julian said it was gruesome. He would've asked Kendra but, yesterday, her eyes, swollen and bloodshot, made him recede. He noticed a pain that, even during their sunny trip, proved difficult to conceal. Julian seemed better at hiding his grief. Alone in his office, there were moments when Julian's grip clenched. Then, loosened around the pen, a tapping that echoed through the room. His gaze fixated on a chess piece, the knight, on the desk. A relic in brother rivalry and a test of wits but rooted in shared respect. David tried stepping into the office-- he paused. He realized his entry would only provoke displeasure. Now, like Julian, David's hands clenched, feet anchored to the floor and unable to enter this sacred moment. He wanted to at least embrace, talk to him-- something. Yet, he could do nothing. In the midst, David's mind shifted to the other family members also dealing with a loss.

David slowed by the zoo, pointing towards the black steel lion statue atop the podium. Shifting his attention from Kendra who grinned, David observed her son. Ethan, lost in his music, seemed oblivious. Soon after, the teen glanced up, huffed, then proceeded to scroll through his phone. David shrugged it off, assuming Ethan was too old for childish attractions.

Now the car was at a complete stop. David gazed at the lion, but behind the structure something caught his attention. He glanced at Kendra, hoping she saw it too, but her eyes were on the lion. Ethan, with eyes sealed shut, remained immersed in his music. David sat up straight, searching again, but it vanished. The scorching sun, he suspected, had beguiled his vision with a mirage.

"Let's visit Charlene and Zek" Kendra turned to him.

David wasn't sure about visiting them. The last visit ended on the brink of shedding blood. For this reason, Julian preferred no contact, even urging him to stay away. David chose not to, even if Julian said he shouldn't. He didn't want Charlene and Zek at the house either, but Chrystal could visit on occasions.

David considered Julian's sister tolerable, when she refrained from constant fighting with everyone. He pondered on her hateful emotions; a burden that left him heartbroken. No one should harbor such anger without a reason. There had to be an explanation.

As much as he sympathized, being in her presence drained him. In truth, he enjoyed the company of Chrystal's daughter over hers. Whereas Julian seemed to tolerate his sister and Lanna, along with Ethan. David held no judgment toward the nephew, besides pity. A reserved teen who rarely spoke to David. Yet, he thought of Ethan's mother and himself as best friends. While Kendra married into Julian's favor. David assumed Julian respected his deceased brother's decisions. Despite the relative that passed, he disliked how the family treated Julian. He wished they could be nicer to each other.

In the midst of these thoughts, Kendra stared at David as if waiting for an answer. He didn't want to say no since he didn't want her smile to fall. In the rear mirror, he noticed Ethan appeared attentive to the conversation. David wondered if the visit might ease the teen's mind. He was silent for a moment, staring into space. In his mind, he considered staying for a minute, hoping to understand Charlene and Zek.

David forced a smile, gripping the steering wheel. "Yeah sure. Why not?" The words escaped his lips, almost stumbling out.

After passing the zoo, he turned right and drove by a grocery store. It was warm outside; many people were shopping or enjoying the weather. Like these people, he hoped Charlene and Zek weren't home. After a few minutes on the road, they finally arrived at the house. A bit small, modest, and traditional– reminiscent of a forgotten chapter in history. It had trimmed grass, and the hedges by the window were a healthy green. The old bricks held history, with cracks, or unforgettable memories. A breeze played notes on an antique wind chime. A chair, dating back to King Jr's era, rocked back and forth on the porch.

While the chair swayed, it thrashed as a rabbit bolted from the porch. David observed the rabbit's frantic escape, pondering the cause of its abrupt terror. Then, he noticed a creature with fur that was a shade of stone. With a glimpse, he could tell something felt unnatural about its eyes, glowing like hell fire. He only glanced, so as to avoid its gaze. Yet, he could sense the creature staring at him, a feeling that knotted his stomach. Then, what seemed like a fox had vanished behind the house. David sat back, letting the air escape from his lips. He'd never seen a fox, but the creature didn't match his expectations. David darted his eyes between Kendra and Ethan, but they seemed relaxed.

David sighed again. Ignoring the incident, though he questioned if this visit affected his perception of reality. Despite the concern, he still parked in front of the fence. Kendra was the first to get out, then Ethan, and last David.

"Can't stay too long! Julian's cooking dinner!" David shouted to them, dragging behind, and waiting.

Kendra rushed to the door and knocked. It opened to reveal Zek on the other side. *Great—* David thought. It had to be this guy.

When thinking of Zek, the first image that came to David's mind was three white lines. One line for himself, the second for the stripper he took home, and the third to save for later. He hated to admit but David thought of Zek as a roach, a dirty pest. Yet, somehow women wanted to sleep with the scumbag. The man smelt of ashtrays and cheap cologne. When drunk, his grammar was poor as if he spoke like a child. Zek's lips, like his fingers, were black and the skin inside his elbow had bruised needle marks. His arms were veiny and muscular because of the toxins in his bloodstream. On one arm was a tattoo of a rabbit in a magician's hat. Zek never told anyone what it meant but he claimed the chicks loved it. David assumed someone trashy would enjoy the display. It should be noted that most women tolerated Zek's drinking; but when faced with harder drugs, they often ran. David paused— lingering on the isolation embedded in those words. Zek had married euphoria, somehow comforted by its addictive embrace. No woman could measure, or they never competed. It was either them or the pills, but Zek never chose the women. From what Julian said, not even the family could end the toxic relationship with the drugs. Zek's addiction climaxed to almost killing his sister.

Once, Chrystal had misplaced a box with drugs, leading Zek to suspect her of stealing. David recalled Zek foaming at the mouth, fixated on her. He lunged, while Julian and Lanna tried to pry his hands from Chrystal's throat. After that moment and similar ones, David avoided Zek.

Smelling like liquor, Zek leaned over to hug Kendra, who returned a hearty embrace. Yet, Zek side-eyed David, offering him a brief nod in passing. David sighed, with arms crossed, returning a subtle gesture. Meanwhile, Zek fist-bumped Ethan, prompting David to roll his eyes before heading inside.

Upon entering, the house looked like an antique store. Above the limestone fireplace, shelves showcased ceramic baby Jesus figurines. The living room's wallpaper featured an elegant vine pattern. Plastic-covered couches resembled dollhouse furniture. Even the vase by the couch and the plants were plastic.

The wood on the grandfather clock also appeared fake, contributing to the gloss. Everything seemed authentic but masked a facade. Although, one thing was real—the aroma from the kitchen. David smelled fried catfish, collard greens, and cornbread. Down the hallway, sizzling hissed nearby.

"Ma-ama! Guess… who's heere?" Zek slurred while stumbling on his feet.

"No whores bettah be in my house... Oops. 'Scuse me, darlin'." Charlene rushed over to Ethan, pinching and kissing on his cheeks. "Hey, give me sum suga' baby!"

Charlene's gaze shifted to Kendra, then she shuffled over with a smile, giving a heartfelt hug. For a moment, Kendra tensed but then eased into the embrace. David considered the interaction, a strange behavior from Kendra, but he let it slip his mind.

David watched as Charlene peered over Kendra's shoulders, greeting him with a brief wave.

Avoiding eye contact, Charlene forced her lips to curl. "David, you droppin' 'em off?"

Kendra pulled David in closer. "We were exploring the town— it's stunning. But Ethan insisted on visiting his grandma. Plus, I've always wanted to see the house; it's beautiful."

David noticed the old lady smiled. Yet, Charlene and Zek had shared a glance. An expression more surprised than concerned. David hoped it hinted at not kicking out Kendra along with him.

Charlene smiled, as genuine as her furniture, and led them to the kitchen. On the counters, there were no signs of cooking. The flour huddled in the bowl, as if fearing Charlene's punishment for messing up her counters. Meanwhile, the grease sizzled in the skillet, not daring to pop, as if dreading Charlene's lethal glare if it stained her walls. The only evidence of cooking was the food on the dining room table. Everyone sat down at the table while Charlene went into the kitchen. Once she came back, the old lady had a jug and cups.

"Iced tea?" Charlene handed Zek the glasses to distribute. "Y'all oughta stay for supper – and David too, if he's game." A smile crept on her face, avoiding David's gaze.

David, stepping in front of Kendra, strained a smile. "Sorry, can't stay. Julian is cooking, your son, remember? But maybe another time, perhaps."

Charlene squinted, wrinkling her nose and recoiling away as she glanced at him. He didn't understand her expression– well, at least not quite.

At the time he yearned to grasp Zek's experience with his affliction. Yet, David had cussed him out, growing fed-up with the drunk targeting

Julian. This happened when Julian came around more which, back in the day, still wasn't often. He recalled Charlene asking Julian for Zek's rehab money. Why not, David had thought. After all, they were Zek's Family. No, after Julian's refusal, he understood the denial of the request. The mother's and brother's words dripped with cruelty. Each syllable deteriorated the fragile bonds, leaving only hatred. Much of it seeped from unsettled debts. The venom of bitter remarks, and disgusting slurs had simmered, threatening a brawl. Rather than staying, Julian grabbed David and slammed the door on their way out.

Even now, the incident seemed to linger. Zek set his glass farther away, avoiding David's hands. Zek's clenched fist appeared to hold resentment. As she poured the drinks, Charlene nodded at Zek, a silent agreement between mother and son. When she poured David's drink, she smirked, invading his space.

Whatever she thought, it must've been ignorant-- she was always prejudiced.

"H-how's the princess?" Zek loomed over David, the stench of liquor spilling from his crooked grin.

"Princess? Are we talking about Lanna? I think she's fine, right?" Kendra whispered with a half-smile, tilting her head to the side.

Zek's attempt at humor, calling Julian a princess, had never failed to itch his patience. David thought about tearing into Zek with vile words-- shoving the drunk away. Yet, he didn't since he had to avoid more problems for Julian, and aware he wasn't supposed to be at Charlene's house. Instead, he turned to the window, overlooking the street, thinking he should've stayed in the car. If Julian found out, the aftermath wouldn't end well-- nagging him about his decisions. Julian's anger, at least most of it, wouldn't be at David but instead directed toward the situation. In either case, David kept quiet, fiddling with his glass.

"He still ain't married you? Hmm, seems like a phase to me– a long one. But maybe that's for the best, darlin'. It's, um, let's say– unnatural." Charlene sipped her tea. Then, she turned, smiling at Zek who exchanged a drowsy smile.

Tapping the glass cup, David resisted letting them affect him. Yet this time, Charlene's remark hit a nerve. She didn't know anything! David knew Julian loved him, but– he needed time, and David understood the wait. From Charlene, the mother, Julian learned to mistrust and to guard his heart; so, David waited. Soon, both of them would find their happy ending.

Charlene waited for a response, then resumed sipping her iced tea as silence lingered. In front of Charlene, Ethan's widened eyes hinted at a newfound awareness of the family. The teen nudged his drink away, settling the headphones atop his head. David, from across the table, noticed Kendra's gaze, processing the situation. She seemed on the verge of saying something...

David shot up from his chair. "We should leave." He abandoned the full glass on the table. Yeah, he had enough.

"Wait, can't we all get along?" Kendra watched as David walked away.

Kendra looked even more confused but stood with him. Ethan, willing to follow behind his mother, rushed to the front door as Charlene chased after them. Zek, slouching on the couch, took a metal flask from his pocket and poured something into his iced tea. He sighed, looking out the window.

Outside, before Charlene could protest, David had slammed the car door. Charlene tried another attempt of redemption, hugging Kendra, but she recoiled. As Kendra turned around, David noticed her tense posture. He wondered if Kendra had ever shown affection to Charlene before the visit.

"Wait! Don't you take my son, ugh, I mean— my grandson away from me. He's all I have left. Please, Kendra!" Charlene's eyes searched Kendra for sympathy, seeing if her words had an effect— they didn't.

Charlene then extended her arms toward Ethan. Yet, he averted her gaze, immersing himself in the music's embrace. A subtle sting grazed the old lady's face, lingering, as Ethan hurried towards the waiting SUV. Once Ethan and Kendra got in the car, David drove away, clenching the wheel.

On the road, his thoughts lingered at Charlene's place, replaying her comment. Yet, he dismissed it, smiling and turning up the radio. He noticed Kendra staring, with concern, but David raised the radio's volume before she spoke. Charlene had a flawed understanding of love and care. He shouldn't take advice from someone who couldn't maintain a relationship. Nonetheless, with her children, she tried her best but could've done more. Better yet, he should've headed straight home from the start.

CHAPTER 7

In the Kitchen, Julian with a sleek bald fade and a well-tailored suit had put on an apron. He sliced herbs with clean cuts and snapped the pasta in half, tossing it in boiling water. In another pan, Julian sprinkled a perfect blend of garlic, oregano, and red pepper flakes. He had his spices imported since he refused the defective produce in the stores. As the herbs sizzled, he raised a brow and hummed, knowing that his ancestors would be proud. Turning to the smartphone, he swiped to the next ingredient-- shrimp.

He casted it in the pan, infusing the kitchen with a rich aroma of garlic, creamy butter, and Old Bay seasoning. Whereas the businessman, and now a chef, smelt like cologne from Dubai and incense from China.

Checking the time on his phone, Julian noticed it was getting late. He glanced at the device again— no messages from David. He thought nothing of it, since David must've lost track of time, but he wondered about his whereabouts. Despite the absence, the food wasn't done, rendering it a trivial concern.

Julian began collecting plates for the table. As he turned to glance at the sunset, he checked the time again. Now, plates were set, and food was almost done. Ever since this morning, he thought about preparing pasta and shrimp for tonight. Uncertain if Kendra and Ethan would enjoy it, he decided they ate or starved. It's too late to order Italian food—although that new restaurant would've been nice. Yet, he was trying to be a good host because David convinced him. It didn't matter. Julian preferred cooking for David, Kendra, and Ethan. While the labor of cooking for others, Ezekiel in particular, revealed burdensome. Dealing with people in general proved to be a task.

Yesterday, before Ethan and Alanna came back to the house, his addict brother arrived. At first, he waited inside for Ethan, while Kendra and David stood outside. They heard about the panic attack, searching for Lanna's truck. Yet, Charlene's car arrived first, and Ezekiel stumbled out. He watched as Ezekiel dragged across the grass, staggering toward the house. The addict had an unsteady stride as if he owned the lawn. He anticipated Ezekiel begging for cash but didn't expect the addict during this time of day. Ezekiel usually came to borrow early morning or late at night. This made Julian a bit nervous because he wasn't sure what his addict brother had planned. If Charlene hadn't intervened, Julian would have shot the trespassing addict. Then again, he should've shot her for bringing Ezekiel to his house.

Julian jerked his head toward the living room. Something had shattered on the floor. He paused— for a heartbeat, waiting for something to move. As the silence crept, he grabbed a knife and his phone, running to the front door. His gun was upstairs, but the knife would work. Well, that's if the intruder didn't have a gun.

Julian stopped by the living room entrance. Near a broken window, the pieces of a vase and glass had scattered across the floor. With a raised brow, Julian walked over, picking up a brick from the debris. Tied around the block was a note that read:

Leave this neighborhood, or else.

Sincerely, The Sunny Fields Community.

Julian grunted, thinking about tossing the note, but shoved it in his pocket. He needed evidence in case the police actually investigated. He never trusted them to do their job, but especially the ones in the south. He glanced around the room, searching for anything else broken. Then, he noticed paw-like prints, ash-colored, as if an animal had walked through flames. Julian assumed a critter had smelled food and jumped through the window to get in the house. Yet, his gaze lingered on the jagged frame, noticing a patch of gray fur. The wildlife was his other reason for hating the neighborhood, besides the people. Even after this, David might insist on staying.

Julian glimpsed a shadow dash across the hallway. He thought he saw gray, like a fog, but it vanished too fast for him to tell. Though it appeared as an animalistic entity, leaving a trail of fur behind. He wished a raccoon, or a cat would jump out. Whereas the chill on his spine whispered a sinister presence had invited itself.

Julian swung toward the bathroom at the sound of scratching against the walls. Julian scrolled through his phone, searching for animal control. Sometimes he didn't trust that they were helpful. Yet, the web browser displayed 'No WiFi'. He assumed an unseen force had severed his connection to the outside world. He wondered if David had called, and he didn't know.

Julian walked down the hallway, fearing the intruder's threat to his sacred space. This house embodied the results of hard work, even when no one else believed in him. The thought of losing it was unbearable, a weight heavier than any other burden he carried. In that moment, he realized that he cherished this house more than the family it protected him from. The bond ran deeper than blood, a testament to the sacrifices within these walls. The corridors echoed with Dreams and memories of this home. He wouldn't lose something so dear. He would fight with every inch of his body before surrendering.

He gripped the knife, seeing claw marks covering the walls of the hallway, even the ceiling. The small prints in the living room were different from the large jagged grooves. Following the trail, the tracks led to the bathroom. Once the prints disappeared, he saw eyes like hellish flames staring in the darkness. Something started to snarl, causing him to step back. The creature, though fox-sized, emitted an unnatural bellow that made his chest tremble. Somehow, the creature suffocated him in its cryptic void. He felt any movement might lead to jaws on his neck. Gripping the knife, he moved the blade in front of him as he watched those eyes sink to the floor. Julian struggled to see the creature, but it seemed to crouch, ready to strike. He paused— As he stared into darkness, his breath became trapped in his throat. His body imitated rigor mortis, locking his steps. Those eyes, older than the sun, fixated on him. Despite the knife's blade, the ancient force casted doubt in his mind.

"Don't be afraid sweetheart. It's me." A distorted voice echoed from the darkness.

"Aunt Lydia...?" Julian whispered.

"We're home!" Kendra yelled.

Julian turned in Kendra's direction and then back around. The fiery eyes had disappeared. He rushed to the living room. The paw prints were gone but pieces of the vase were on the floor. At least, he didn't imagine that part. Yet, he was certain that his mind conjured that voice, because she was dead.

"What the hell happened here?" David stomped into the room and slammed the window. Julian tried to meet David's gaze, but it seemed David avoided eye contact. While attempting to study his behavior, Julian felt hindered by the earlier horror.

Julian loosened his grip on the knife. "Mississippi wind can move houses; a vase ain't no exception. Now, if you'll 'scuse me, I oughta sweep, not chatter 'bout trivial matters. Ugh, where's the maid when we need her?" Julian's laugh trembled.

David seemed to strain his grin, staring into space. Another odd expression he noticed. Despite this, Julian laughed, running and searching for a broom. He thought about keeping the bathroom incident to himself. Even if he said something, he didn't trust that they would believe him.

Then, Kendra rushed to the smoke from the kitchen. Damn! He forgot about the food! He raced behind Kendra as she turned the stove off. They salvaged a few shrimps before they all turned into black horseshoes. Julian turned toward David in the hallway, still in a daze. He wondered if anything happened while they were out. David stayed composed, rarely letting things affect him. Yet, when David got angry, even Julian hesitated to approach. So, he decided to ignore the strangeness, for the moment— and finished dinner.

Once the pasta was ready, he served everyone in the dining room, where they sat down in silence. With the first bite, he found the food lacking, blaming it on overcooking. Now, with a clear mind, he noticed the stillness of everyone's fork. They ate— with slow, silent bites— avoiding eye contact. Even Kendra, who always had something to say, was mute. From their reactions, it was clear something had gone wrong on their trip. As David stabbed at his noodles, Julian sensed he wouldn't like what he was about to hear. He bit into a shrimp— it tasted bitter. Despite everyone's disgusted expression, Julian doubted it was because of the taste. He wondered if asking would reveal the issue.

"How was the trip 'round town?" Julian scanned the room. A silence loomed over the table.

"It was good." Kendra smiled, glancing at David.

Julian raised a brow, his gaze shifting between Kendra and David. He knew they were hiding something.

"We saw Granny," Ethan replied, looking down at his plate.

Then David glanced at Julian, fidgeting as if in trouble, which held some truth. Julian huffed, dropping his fork on the table, and visualizing the incident. David should've known why they avoided Charlene and Ezekiel. Last time, Julian punched Ezekiel, who mistook David's kindness with flirtation. Then, he cut off Charlene for kicking him out at 12, leaving him with his aunt.

He loved his aunt: her cunning, lavish style, and work ethic. He felt that she was the only person he could depend on. He missed her, being that years have vanished since her passing. No one else seemed to care, except him, David, and Ethan's father who embraced Julian as he cried over her casket. He wondered if the tears came from her death, or the fact that most of the family didn't show. At least his aunt's sister, Charlene, should've come.

Recalling from heated arguments, his deadbeat father abandoned Charlene for someone else. This led to her yelling at Aunt Lydia, who confessed the man had never loved her. Explaining inconsistencies on his father's part— whatever that meant. He never met the man, so he wasn't sure. Regardless, his aunt took him in, a possible tactic for revenge against her sister.

Sometimes, he also believed his aunt protected him from his father's sins— a darkness. Yeah, Aunt Lydia was superstitious like that. Both Charlene and Aunt Lydia prayed. In fact, Aunt Lydia would've rebuked the entity from the bathroom. Charlene, otherwise, would burst into flames, touching holy water.

Whenever he saw Charlene, that wicked hag, Julian wished she had died of cancer instead of Aunt Lydia. His aunt would've scolded him for that comment, but he didn't care.

Charlene favored his older siblings over him. She especially catered to Ezekiel and Ethan's father. Julian also noticed Charlene's favoritism towards Chrystal, whom she kicked out as well. At least she waited for Chrystal to turn 18, hinting at some sense of guilt on her mother's part. Yet, Charlene, his mother as well, didn't seem guilty for kicking him out. Before Aunt Lydia saved him, he experienced homelessness.

His siblings lived in plenty while Julian ate scrapes. He slept on concrete pillows and cardboard sheets.

As a child, Julian remembered adult hands wrapped around his thin neck. His lungs began to suffocate under the man's weight, fighting with every inch of his bony body. Julian looked up at the man foaming from the mouth, his feral eyes harbored murder.

No humanity. No trust.

The man only understood starvation, eyeing Julian's bag of chips. The man grabbed his wrist, digging into the flesh of his hand.

The mad man yanked. Julian shoved.

Yet, as a starving child, he didn't have the strength to escape.

The grown man punched. Julian blocked.

Julian could feel his arms bruising, flesh tearing from huge knuckles. He turned his head, noticing a screwdriver on the ground.

The wild man snapped like a serpent.

Julian felt the man's breath on his neck, threatening to break skin, but the man paused. Julian released the bloody tool, hands trembling as he freed himself from dead weight. The man was dead, but Julian still had what already belonged to him.

As he sat at the table, scanning his dining room, he sighed. Julian wondered if Charlene would've rescued him if she ever knew. Then again, he believed he resembled one of her scars, from her husband, that never healed. Sometimes he felt as if none of them would've saved him. For this reason, he preferred to avoid the family who deserted him.

At the table, Julian raised a brow at David, opening his mouth but ate noodles instead. He thought about trying later, seeing that his nephew and Kendra were at the table. He relaxed his brow, eating at a steady pace, and strategizing his private talk with David. Julian felt angrier with Charlene but still harbored some resentment towards David. He loved him. Even though his sweet but naïve partner always tried to see the best in others. Yet, Julian knew firsthand about trusting the wrong people.

When Kendra started talking about the statue at the zoo, Julian leaned in closer. Analyzing the rest of their trip, and David. After dinner, Kendra and Ethan went upstairs for bed. David stayed downstairs with Julian to finish washing the dishes. At first David scrubbed, looking down at the sink, then glanced at Julian. David's lips twitched as if suppressing words.

"They wanted to see her..." David wiped the fork.

"They treated us horrible, but you're still fixin' to set that right, ain't ya?" Julian clenched a spoon.

"Yeah, I know, but um, they're—you know. Well, ugh. They're like family."

"Really?! Family?" Julian threw the spoon in the water.

Sickened by David's unrealistic ideologies, he wished the man would wake up. Family was only a word people used for exploitation.

Julian sighed, leaning against the counter. No one saw the world like him. In those streets, and as a child, he saw human's true nature. People, including his family, were ignorant and selfish with no empathy for others. Julian hated that reality. That's why he wanted Kendra and Ethan to leave before they treated him like Ezekiel did. He never understood why the drunk hated him, but it began when Julian turned 12. He always felt Chrystal held secrets, but Ezekiel did too. They hid things about themselves, Charlene and their father.

Julian jerked his head toward the doorway. He thought he heard something snarl. Yet, David didn't seem to react to the sound. Julian stared into the darkness, as a chill clawed up his spine.

"I don't want to fight!" David slammed a plate into the sink. A trickle of blood dripped from his hand.

Julian reached over to the drawer and pulled out a first aid kit. He took David's hand and began cleaning the cut. After Julian bandaged the wound, he and David gathered the shards.

Julian looked over to David. "I don't trust'em. But I have faith in you. Okay?"

Julian grinned watching as David nodded his head with a smile. Julian didn't mention the paw prints or the thing in the bathroom, but he kept glancing at the dark hallway. David, who didn't seem to notice this new tic, washed another plate. It didn't seem Kendra heard the plate break or arguing because she would've ran down the stairs. Yet, in case she was listening, they cleaned the dishes in silence.

CHAPTER 8

Through the window, the warm sunlight illuminated the space. Inside the room, some flowering plants casted shadows across the carpet to the bed. The rug was green, resembling moss after an April shower. The bed covers were fluffy like clouds on a spring day, while the pillows were an earthy tone. The walls were a bleached white and the ceilings were a hue of dove feathers.

Almost bird-like, Kendra glided over to the dresser and picked up a strand of fur. She paced, searching for more, having already found similar pieces around the house. David claimed a stray cat came by sometimes, making her wonder if they had let the dirty feline inside. Kendra dropped the fur and rubbed in sanitizer until her hands turned red. Kendra gagged, thinking of the diseases she touched. She thought for a place that had a maid, it wasn't too clean. Yesterday, Kendra noticed something black, like ashes, on the kitchen counter. She had taken a towel and wiped it off.

Despite her complaints, helping around the house showed her gratitude for their shelter. She didn't know where they'd be without Julian and David. Even though Julian pushed away, not appreciating her hard work. She felt exhausted without any thanks in return.

Kendra collapsed on the bed, feeling silken sheets on her skin. As she sank, an odd sensation embraced her. A pleasure she hadn't allowed herself to experience since— Marquis, her husband, died.

Kendra twisted to the right. She thought of the first time she met Marquis Hare. She believed it was English 101 because that course started in the morning, first class of the year. He had a cup of coffee with cream and no sugar, the way he liked it.

She turned in the bed now staring at a plaid jacket on the chair. The jacket had a few torn stitches and holes. She remembered how good he looked in it. Marquis wore the same jacket that day, carrying his coffee and books for the class. Her attention should've been on the professor, but Kendra couldn't stop staring at Marquis's face. From the side, his cheek bones guided her gaze to his lips which she wanted to touch. She imagined the man in a plaid jacket might feel like her first kiss, or better.

On the covers, Kendra shifted her body again. She admitted to staring too long, and Marquis caught her. She reminisced the way he looked at her. A blush made her appear nervous, but this wasn't the case. Seeing that his eyes appeared as a comfort, a warm smile, making the world soften around her. He grinned, as if captivated by her beauty too. Now, she missed the way he looked at her.

She clenched the pillow, trembling within its cotton. The bed felt like cold clay, a sensation that suffocated her. Marquis's death weighed on her heart, and this bed offered no peace.

Kendra stood up.

She walked to the chair where Marquis's jacket laid, noticing one sleeve hanging from the armrest. Kendra folded the plaid jacket, ensuring each crease aligned, before placing it on the bed.

Then, she turned around and sat in the chair. She gazed, fixated on the mirror atop the dresser. It had a gold frame with babies carved into the metal. Pictures of babies with angel wings depicted them playing music and laughing. The mirror, a clear reflection of the truth, revealed Kendra's face. She needed some makeup. Kendra took out her supplies and started getting to work.

First, she used a quick mist and a cool cream to get started, something refreshing. Then Kendra applied a foundation, so she wasn't burdened with mistakes later on. She applied concealer to hide imperfections, like signs of restless nights. To add flare, she used eyeshadow, to attract attention to her eyes rather than the shadows under them. Her favorite part, the lipstick, made everything cohesive. She used a shade of purple, African violet. After puckering her lips, she stared into the mirror.

Though the transformation was complete, her watery eyes appeared ugly. Kendra pivoted to the bed where the plaid jacket rested. Then, as her eye shadow trickled down her cheeks, she conjured his image, seated upon the bed. She yearned for his presence, longing for his voice to declare her beauty.

She knew Ethan grieved his father, but she wasn't sure about everyone else. At the time Kendra's focus was on her son; but she never considered how it might've affected Marquis's siblings. Julian seemed more distant from the family while Zek was a pill away from death. Even though she and Chrystal haven't had a recent conversation, something felt off. When Lanna and Chrystal dropped off Ethan, Chrystal's fury chiseled her face into stone. Lanna also appeared irritated. Mama remained steady, but the family had struggled, thinking of Marquis's death.

She noticed her phone next to his worn-out jacket. A solution began to illuminate in her mind. Then, she turned to her reflection. Again, she admired the embedded artwork on the mirror's gold frame. Seeing how they enjoyed each other's presence. She should get the family together like that. Kendra pushed the chair aside and then reached for the phone. She started dialing in her sister-in-law's number.

Kendra connected her headphones. "Hello...? Chrystal...?"

Chrystal sighed. "Yeah, whatcha want?"

"Nothing, Um, I was seeing how things were going, with you, Lanna-- and the baby. Is Lanna okay?" Kendra started brushing her hair.

"Um, yeah? Lanna could do better. She's fixin' to git rid of it."

Kendra paused. "Hmm, why?"

"Dunno, but she's bein' selfish." Chrystal's voice shifted into a whisper. "She ain't like me, I'm tellin' ya. Ugh, fuckin' self-centered."

"Why say that?" Kendra receded back to brushing.

"Forget it. It ain't none of your business." Chrystal tone sizzled as if the phone would melt.

Kendra brushed slower. "Sorry-- Well, I had an idea, if you care to know, for a baby shower. Maybe, a party will change her mind. Also, surrounded by family, don't you think?"

"If she'll listen. Lanna's scared."

"I understand. I felt scared with Ethan. We both know that raising children isn't for the weak. But don't worry, I'll talk to her today."

"You will?" Chrystal's voice raised, jumping from the other end of the phone.

"Yup, I got everything under control. I'll text the information."

"Countin' on you. Don't fuck it up!" The call ended.

Kendra hesitated as she dialed, wary of alarming her niece by revealing the true purpose of the call. However, Lanna didn't answer. So instead, Kendra texted about a family get-together. She mentioned it could ease Ethan's nerves, which was half true. Her niece texted back-- *Great idea*-- with a heart emoji. Kendra smiled, pleased with her plan's progress. Now she had to call Mama and Zek.

During their recent visit to Mama's house-- with David, Ethan, and her-- she had sensed tension in the room. David displayed an emotion that she had never seen from him-- hatred. She harbored a distaste for Mama as well, though she buried her pride for her son. Kendra felt something had transpired between

Julian, David, Mama, and Zek. When they came back home, Julian appeared upset when Ethan mentioned visiting Mama. A brief glimpse of rage crossing his face before vanishing. Whereas David's mind seemed to wander off. She figured the conflict sparked from the two men's relationship. Kendra believed Mama's remarks held resentment toward her ex-husband. Yet, Zek had no reason for hostility that she could perceive.

She wondered if the grief surrounding Marquis's death had fueled the family's turmoil. After leaving the funeral early, this party could serve as an emotional outlet. Then again, babies bring people together. She imagined David mixing cocktails, Ethan DJing, Mama and Julian cooking (a redo on his pasta). Then, Zek staying sober, Lanna relaxing, and Chrystal teaching everyone to dance. It was molding into the perfect party.

Kendra started dialing mama's number. The phone rang.

#

The house phone rang. Charlene gasped as she entered the living room, her heart skipping a beat at the sight of Zek sprawled on the floor. The stillness of his body sent a shiver down her spine until she noticed a faint movement. A subtle twitch of his finger had shattered the illusion of death. This wasn't the first time she found her idiot son in this condition. He overdosed once in the kitchen, vomiting on the tiles. Again, she found him on the floor, assuming he was high but safe. Seeing the liquor on the table, she realized he'd drunk himself to sleep instead of sweeping. Also, the gutters on the roof, which she had mentioned to him two weeks ago, were still clogged with gunk. Yet, she shouldn't expect much from a lazy moron.

Charlene threw a pillow. "Get up! Ya makin' a mess in mah livin' room."

No response.

She sighed, seeing he thought of nothing better to do but lounge around. He wasn't at work because he got fired for using drugs in the restroom. Now, he was unemployed on top of being a high school dropout. Charlene thought about throwing him out a long time ago, but the men in white coats took him. Then again, she knew he couldn't live on his own even if he tried. After rehab, Zek claimed he had found a job and brought home a suspicious amount of cash. She ignored the signs, never asking too many questions. This seemed like his first steps into manhood, but she still feared the police breaking down her door.

The phone rang again.

Seeing that Zek was unable, Charlene stepped over him to answer the phone. "Hey, this is the Hare's house. Who's callin'?"

"Hey, it's me-- Kendra. I wanted to plan something for the family."

"Mmm, what ya thinkin'? An' who all's comin'?" Charlene squinted.

"It's a family get-together with everyone, can you come?"

"I dunno...Might jus' make thangs worse." Charlene looked over at Zek groaning on the rug.

"Julian wants you to come."

"Julian? Wanna see me?" Charlene took a seat.

"Yes, said it himself. So, I'll text Zek the date."

Charlene glanced at Zek again. "Julian wanna see Zek too? I wouldn't blame him if he didn't, but he should, at least, want me over. I'm his mama."

"Of course! I think Julian feels scared to talk about his feelings. Oh, there won't be alcohol."

"Mmm, reckon he figured out what's best. Okay, I'll get Zek to send me the info."

"Yup, see you there. Bye, bye."

"Bye sweetheart." Charlene hung up.

Charlene turned to the man she called her son on the floor. Then she kicked him in the ribs. With that, he shot up, eyes red with dark circles under them.

"Ouch...!" Zek rubbed the sore spot on his side, almost teary eyed.

He sounded injured, but Charlene sat down, glaring at him. She thought he'll get over it. Now she rolled her eyes, watching him stare back as if she did something wrong. Well, she didn't, so he needed to toughen up and act like a man. She hadn't raised him to be like her ex-husband. Sometimes she loathed how much he looked like his father. As she sat in the chair, she had the urge to smack that puzzled expression off Zek's face. Being that her husband looked the same when she caught him. When she discovered her ex-husband in their bed, the sight had curdled her stomach. Her ex-husband had let in the sin of sexual immorality into their bedroom. Now glaring at her son, she felt the same nausea. Zek's lips, as if a baby pouting, added to his dim-witted expression. Zek had a look of ignorance like trying to understand why the square didn't roll. She wondered how long she could endure his wimpy behavior. Although Charlene felt blessed not to deal with her ex-husband. After he left, she no longer had to take care of another woman in men's clothes. A lady like herself needed a real man in the house.

"Why did ya do that?" Zek whined.

"Boy, that ain't nothin' compared to the pain I done been through. Try givin' birth to someone with a big head like yours." Charlene threw another pillow at him. "Be a man and do somethin' 'round here instead of gettin' high and eatin' up my grub. And pick up mah pillows."

"I'm tired of this, sh— crap! You'll regret when I leave." Zek whimpered, massaging his rib.

"Leave!? Ha, you done said'em words 20-damn-years-ago. How 'bout you leave now, since you don't appreciate all I've done for you. I gave birth to *you*, I paid for your rehab, and *y'all* had food on the table. It was ALL ME! Not sum good-for-nothin' who can't even hold a job." Charlene huffed, throwing her purse at him, "When's Ezekiel goin' to pay me back for everything he took from me, huh?"

Zek grunted, standing up with a gradual push and a clenched jaw as he wiped his eyes. Charlene's face twisted as she looked away. He didn't have anything to be sad about. After her ex-husband left, she worked overtime to ensure Zek, and his siblings had their needs. Yet, Chrystal thought she was grown with a baby at 13, Julian played with dolls, and Zek shot up drugs. She wondered if her other son, Marquis, would've had any surprises for her. Then, she wondered if she did something wrong. She was a great mother for the situation they were in. Her husband left them when she was pregnant with the youngest of her children, Juian, but she didn't turn to drugs. Zek had everything, but still popped pills, disrespecting all her hard work. She watched as he picked up the pillows and appeared on the verge of crying like a man child. She rolled her eyes again, thinking he needed to grow up.

"Jus' like yo' daddy– He couldn't be a man neither."

Zek stormed around Charlene and swung open the door. Then, the house shook as the door slammed behind him.

CHAPTER 9

From the entrance, Zek could smell liquor and sweaty fishnets. He walked past the half-naked woman and her customer with a stack of cash. Dollar bills flew from the man's hand as she danced in the shower of money. Zek walked by the two. He sat on his stool, requesting his regular drink, no juice or soda to chase. Once the bartender slid his glass to him, Zek turned to scan the scene. A neon sign read, *The Drunken Vixen*. The Vixen was a mixture of a bar and a strip club, both things he enjoyed. Like a regular bar, bottles filled the shelves. Yet, a mirror reflected the entertainment from behind. Under the bottles was the bartender pouring liquor and serving drunken men. Searching around, he noticed none of these men were his friends. And to add, the stage in the middle of the room, with a pole, was empty. Zek sighed, staring down at his glass and filling in his pocket. Well, at least he had his happy powder in his pocket. Toward the far end of the place, Zek noticed the exit to the back alley. He remembered the guys and him would shoot up sometimes on Fridays. They laughed about stupid things and bragged about which stripper they could take to a hotel. Unlike the guys, Zek knew what women wanted. Referring to himself as a player with the best game, he could pick up a gal from anywhere. The guys would chuckle as if Zek made a joke. He'd brush it off because he could prove it. Then after bragging, they would sniff some lines in the bathroom. Yeah, he needed that moment right now, a type of euphoria. Instead of dealing with his mother, he wanted to drown her nagging with alcohol.

He tried to find a job, but it proved impossible. In interviews, they rejected him upon learning of his addiction. Later on, Ezekiel started lying, but that didn't work either. Like mama always said, he found a way to mess up. Yet, he couldn't help letting the drugs win. Most people didn't understand how great it felt, better than sex. Sometimes, it was the only path to his arousal. Right now, he needed something to erect his spirits. Zek took a gulp from his glass.

Zek frowned at the half empty glass, now considering buying shots. As the lights dimmed, he turned toward the stage. The usual show was up there tonight, *Kitty*. She was hideous in the face, like a bulldog, but thick in all the right places. He watched as she spun around the pole like a squirrel looking for a nut. The cash came down like leaves from a tree as she held onto the metal trunk. Same as a sexy warrior, she whipped her hair around. Even though her hair appeared synthetic, he didn't want to ruin the fantasy. Once Kitty finished her dance, the crowd, including Zek, clapped as she left the stage. She did okay and made some cash, but then again there weren't many people in the bar.

Returning to the stage, the announcer started to tease the next show, *Desire*. Zek thought the name sounded interesting, kind of sexy. He was familiar with the names Pop it Polly, or Giggles. Yet, Desire promised something different, something... tempting. He hoped for a performance more captivating than the last.

As the room dimmed again, the spotlight danced on the curtains. From behind the velvet drapes, a curvy leg emerged. Zek paused-- his glass halted half-way to his lips, arrested by the sneak peek. With a caressing motion, she rotated her ankles, uncovering her naked thighs to the crowd. Leaning in, Zek joined the collective anticipation, waiting for Desire to expose herself.

A woman stepped from behind the curtains. Zek thought she looked more like a model than a stripper. Her gorgeous smile made his mouth rise. As he touched his face, he realized that he was grinning. Her eyebrows arched like a feline while her hips slithered like a cobra. He felt intimated, but something about her kept him engaged. Perhaps her swaying hair, or how she walked on her toes had kept him on edge. He almost couldn't breathe as she strolled on the stage, a breath-taking experience. Since her face was triangular, her chin pointed to her breast. He watched them swing while her hip rolled on the pole. Any urge he had to do lines in the bathroom was gone. She was addictive to gaze at.

Desire looked into the crowd. He wondered if she looked at him-- he wished she did. Damnit, she stared at another guy. Zek hated that guy. He wanted her to look at him. Please, stare at him.

Zek walked over to the chair nearest to the stage, next to the man Desire was looking at. With an elegant touch, she grabbed the pole, lifted her beautiful legs, and began swinging. She made her moves seem effortless, as if the pole itself bent to her will. The other men, goggle-eyed, moved their heads to her motions. Having never seen her before, Zek thought she must've been new, but she seemed experienced. She could've been from another city, or very talented. He watched as the woman slowed and tilted her head back. Zek and Desire were now face to face. He wanted her, but he questioned if she wanted him. He almost tried to touch her face, but she pulled away from him. He knew that if he had money, she would stay.

Zek noticed some men leaving their table and walking out. They must've been rich, or stupid, because one of them forgot a stack of a hundred bills on the table. Zek looked around the room to see if anyone was watching. Confirming that everyone had their eyes on Desire, Zek grabbed the money. Then, Desire came back to him again and Zek started throwing the bills hoping they were enough. He wanted to impress this woman. If he had had more money, he would've given it to her. He thought about robbing the register but too many people were around. He didn't care how crazy it seemed; she was worth it. Noticing his recent wealth, she hopped off the stage and settled her thick thighs into Zek's lap.

"Hey, sugah, how you doin'?" She smiled at him with the most gorgeous teeth he had ever seen.

"Great...How...'bout you...?" Zek rubbed the sweat off his hands hoping she didn't notice.

"Want me to show ya a good time?" Desire stared at him, with foxy eyes.

"Yes!" Zek held up the money.

Desire giggled. "Not here, after mah shift? Maybe we can have sum fun at a motel?"

Zek nodded his head. He would go anywhere with her. Was this love? No, be a man and stay focused. Zek held his head up and gripped her waist. Desire must've loved when guys did her like that. Seeming to enjoy his gesture, she winked at him. Yet, like all good strippers, she went back on stage, did a few tricks, and ended her performance. He felt empty like after a high was over. Hating to feel this way, he wanted-- no, needed to see her again. She was his new favorite drug.

Following her instructions, he waited for her outside. For a moment, he thought she had lied to him to get his money, but then she walked out. The woman wore a fox mink coat with high heels. Zek wondered if she wore nothing underneath her coat. As she swayed her hips toward Zek, Desire stared at him with a graceful smile. The excitement was enough to make him collapse, but he stood up straight with his chin held high. Once she was close enough to him, she gave Zek a kiss. It was only on the cheek, but enough for Zek to consider unzipping his pants. Due to her lips feeling like ruffled pillows and messy sheets. He almost melted but remembered he had to maintain his manhood.

"Hey baby. Ready?" Zek deepened his voice.

"Got the money?" She pointed at his pockets.

Zek nodded. Then, Desire gave him a wink, and they headed toward the motel, a strip of fox fur trailing behind them.

CHAPTER 10

Ethan lifted the bed cushion, hoping to find his misplaced belonging, but only found a dollar. After chucking the pillow at the wall, he paused for a minute— trying to recall where he put his headphones. They had blue foam speakers with a sunset design on the sides.

Searching the pockets in his dirty clothes basket, he only found lent. He dug through the sheets on his bed but didn't see it there either. Ethan checked under the bed but only saw the wooden floor and the mattress. He felt for it on the shelf but instead discovered dust on his hands. Ethan searched everywhere in the bedroom but had no luck.

He figured he must have dropped them somewhere else in the house, perhaps the kitchen. Ethan headed down the stairs, smelling bleach as he walked onto shiny floors. In the kitchen, a lady cleaning the counters caught his attention. As she scrubbed, her hands appeared firm like diamonds in their raw form. Her dark skin, like a shade of the night, contrasted with the white apron tied around her waist. While wrapped around her head, she wore a scarf with African patterns. She stopped, noticing him staring. Her eyes reminded him of a leopard's gaze. He stepped closer, not intimidated, but in awe of her enchanting aura. The woman's presence felt different from the rest of the house. The arguments and fake smiles polluted the air, like radiation suffocating his lungs. He couldn't explain why but he could breathe as if the space around her was fresh. Ethan watched the woman wipe her wet hands on her apron, walking toward him.

"You must be Ethan" The lady held her hand out.

Nodding to confirm her assumption, Ethan shook the woman's hand. Her touch felt solid as they appeared, cradling his outstretched palm. Her steady gaze mellowed as she stepped toward him.

"You're... The Maid?" Ethan noticed she smelled like coffee beans and goat meat.

The Maid nodded *yes* to answer. She released Ethan's hand, reaching into her front pocket. Then, she pulled out a pair of blue headphones with a sunset design.

"Is dis yours?" The Maid held out the headphones.

Ethan's eyes widened. "Yes! Thank you!"

The Maid grinned, returning to her cleaning. Yet, she halted, as if almost hitting a bricked wall. Ethan noticed her staring at the floor. Her posture, once relaxed, had now stiffened. His body tensed, but he approached her, following her gaze to paw prints on the tiles. Ethan stepped back, seeing that an animal had tracked black ash into the house. A patch of gray fur clung to the print, as if trapped in tar. This confirmed his suspicions; the fox was hiding somewhere in the house. Ethan scanned the room, but nothing except the paw prints seemed unusual. In his dream, he recalled the creature in a straw hat, its hue reminiscent of the fox's tracks, if not darker. Then, Ethan felt a sensation like bristles of hay raking against his spine, though when he turned, he saw no one. Despite the emptiness, he felt watched, stalked even, as the bloodlust lingered in the air.

The Maid looked at him, as if understanding his trembling fist, which he tried to hide. The lady turned her gaze to the ground as she crouched but avoided touching the paw print. The woman held her hand over the spot, humming a foreign melody, and winced as if her hand had been burnt. She rubbed the tip of her fingers and massaged the palm of her hands. To Ethan's surprise, the woman gestured to him to come closer. Ethan would otherwise have been hesitant, but he felt he could trust her. So, he obeyed, squatting next to The Maid.

"Has any'tin strange happened at this house lately?" The woman glanced at him with intense eyes.

"Well, I've been, um, having weird dreams—Nightmares."

The woman raised a brow and folded her arms. "Like what dreams?"

For some reason, Ethan explained everything to her. From arriving at Uncle Julian's house to now. Ethan paused, checking if The Maid was dialing the number to the psych-ward. Instead, her gaze seemed attentive as if holding on to each word. She asked a few times to describe parts of his nightmare which made him a bit talkative. The feeling seemed strange, but he enjoyed the conversation. He liked the pleasure of comprehension and not only heard. He wondered if she had helped someone else with a similar situation. In fact, who was this woman that Uncle Julian had hired? Ethan noticed a necklace around her neck with an unusual symbol, like an ancient motif. The jewelry reminded him of a witch doctor. She seemed like a typical maid, yet, like the necklace, something about her felt unnatural.

Ethan looked over his shoulder, seeing if any of his family noticed them. Yet, The Maid and him were alone. He continued to check, ensuring that no one was around to eavesdrop. Good thing his mother wasn't in the room. She might force-feed him pills if she heard about a laughing fox or a creature with devilish eyes.

After Ethan finished, The Maid looked up as if stuck in her own thoughts. Then, the woman walked around the kitchen, hands outstretched as if searching. Once she scanned the whole room, she returned to Ethan.

"I t'ink an entity has targeted this family. I sense…wicked intent, and yes, gruesome pain." The Maid closed her eyes, stepping out of the kitchen.

"Like, um, g-ghost…?" Ethan followed her into the living room.

The maid paced around until she stopped at the window. "No…worse…sometin' very ancient, a violent spirit."

"The boogie man?" Ethan watched as she examined the window.

The woman shook her head no. Then, she began gliding her finger across the window frame. She paused at a shelf, where under it, she noticed a shattered vase. After they returned from Granny's house, Ethan recalled Uncle Julian staring at the same vase. Reflecting on dinner, he noticed Uncle Julian's attention drift from the table. As though he appeared disturbed by something beyond the dining room. Ethan couldn't shake the thought: Did Uncle Julian see the fox too?

As Ethan stood there, perplexed by her words, he couldn't help but wonder about her background. She seemed so sure, almost as if she had encountered similar things before. He watched as her hand hovered over the broken vase, her palm steady as oak roots.

Ethan inched closer, joining her by the shelf. "Who are you, really?"

The Maid paused, her gaze shifting to a distant memory. "I am Ayo," she began, as her voice trembled with each word. "I come from Lagos, Nigeria, where I grew up with my two sisters, one brother, and mama."

As she spoke, Ethan noticed a depth in her eyes, a sorrow submerged in discernment and loss.

"Ayo," he whispered back, as if the name held some significance, he couldn't quite grasp.

"I realized at a young age that I could sense things others couldn't," she continued, her tone becoming more somber. "My abilities were passed down from my papa's side of da family, but it came with a heavy burden."

She went on to tell how an evil spirit murdered her father, spurring her on a path of vengeance and into the magic trade. As a child, a shaman, from a rural area

171

outside of Lagos, trained her in the ancient arts of shamanism.

"I've devoted my life to cleansing da spirits," her eyes met Ethan's with a fierce determination. "And I believe da one in this house is da same entity which took papa from me."

Ethan watched as her eyes welled up, a silent testament to her pain. He empathized with her loss, though for him, a spirit didn't take his dad, but something as malicious.

"Now listen, da creature feeds on negative energy— intoxicated by conflict. In ancient times it thrived in civil wars. I know how to stop it, but I need your help, yet only if willin'?"

"Yes! Uh, yeah? I mean yes, I'll help." Ethan touched his face, noticing a grin.

He didn't know how he could assist or what her plan entailed, but he stood prepared for anything. If

Ayo had confidence in her strategy, so did he. The creature and its fox henchmen must leave. He sensed something bad might happen if the creature nested in the house. For now, it was only paw prints and dreams, but soon blood might shed. The woman held out her hand again. Ethan glanced at it and shook it. He thought this was the beginning of a strange friendship.

CHAPTER 11

Kendra stepped out of her room and walked down the hallway until she reached a door. Above her, she noticed a sign that read Office. She tried turning the knob, but the door didn't budge. Assuming Julian had locked it, she huffed. He always seemed trapped in his room, rarely experiencing life beyond its walls.

The upcoming party was for the family, but she believed he needed more. She thought about inviting him for a walk; he might enjoy an open field more than a cramped office. Puffing out her chest and wearing a wide grin, she took a deep breath, sighed, and knocked on the wooden door.

Not hearing anything from the other side, she rolled her eyes, while mumbling David. Given that he claimed Julian should've been in the office since he always worked after breakfast.

Then she gasped, hearing footsteps from the other side. The knob turned and the door opened to reveal Julian peeking out. His tie was loose, crooked; his bald head looked oily; and he smelt like faded, but expensive cologne. She wanted to ask where he bought it, but Julian's expression made her bite her tongue. He raised his brow, with squinted eyes, as if trying to understand why the woman stood at his door.

Attempting to view his office, Kendra stretched her neck. She only caught a glimpse of a desk and camera monitors before Julian blocked her view with his forearm. Now, she thought it might be best to only ask about the party.

"We should throw a baby shower for Lanna" Kendra smiled.

"Lanna wants a baby shower?" Julian kept his brow raised.

"Yes! It'll be fun…I promise"

Julian stared at her for a moment. She wondered if he was deciding to shut the door in her face or kick her out the house. Easing his brow, he stepped from behind the door.

"I dunno…" Julian looked back at his office

"Everyone will be in the backyard. Plus, you need a break from working all the time. I'm sure it would make David happy as well." Kendra watched as Julian appeared to think for a moment.

"Who all did ya invite?" Julian's eyebrow arched.

"Family. So...? Yes...?" Kendra displayed her teeth.

"Hmmm..." Julian squinted at her, searching beyond her smile.

Kendra's smile faded, preparing to explain the true reason for the party. After her son, Ethan, panicked at the grocery store, Kendra felt he was becoming more distant. Julian remained silent, but his expression suggested agreement. Kendra continued by mentioning how the party would ease Ethan's anxiety.

"How's a party gonna help? This here's more serious than a gathcrin' can fix." Julian furrowed his brows, leaning in as he inspected her. "But are you okay?"

Kendra stepped back, avoiding his gaze. "I-I'm fine...I know it won't make him forget about Marquis, but it might help him open up to us. The baby shower will show him, like for Lanna, that we're here for him."

After a moment's stare, Julian's gaze drifted away from her. A weariness not weighed from Kendra's pleads or office hours, but something gnawing at his mind. Kendra noticed his unease since their return from Mama's house. Despite the burnt shrimp, the house seemed unharmed, yet he remained unsettled. For a man of power, confidence, and wealth, something disturbed him at his core.

Julian looked down the hallway, staring at something. "As long as everyone's in the backyard, I don't care."

Kendra followed his gaze but only saw an empty hallway. "Are you okay?"

"Yup." Julian waved goodbye and shut the door.

Kendra looked down the hallway again but saw nothing. She turned toward the door, pausing mid-knock. She wanted to ask what he saw but feared angering him. Instead, she focused on the positive. The plan was coming together. She was mending the family.

Kendra giggled and pranced down the stairs, missing a few steps. Out of the corner of her eye, she noticed a pair of blue headphones on the hallway table. She figured Ethan must've gone into the living room. The thought that Ethan came out of his bedroom on his own made her smile.

As she headed toward the living room, she paused at blood and fur trailing in that direction. She wondered who was bleeding— the stray? No, too much blood for a cat.

Then, she stared back at Ethan's headphones. She thought something might've harmed her child.

She ran into the room. Her breathing felt heavy, her lungs tight, as her eyes darted around the space. She didn't find her son, but she did see a corpse.

Kendra inched toward the source of the blood and fur. A buzzing, like lawnmower blades, came from insects devouring flesh. Larva squirmed through the animal's eyes, gnawing at the empty sockets. The insects buzzed around one long ear while there was a chunk bitten out of the other. Also, guts spilled out where something ripped another chunk of flesh. Blood was everywhere as if the predator had wrung its victim by the throat.

Kendra stepped closer, observing the bite marks on the animal's neck. Something mangled its throat and limbs like a twisted rag doll. She could only identify the rabbit by its bloody ears and matted tail.

Kendra searched the room but couldn't find the rabbit's point of entry. Then, she saw black paw prints lead to the broken window. She assumed the prints were from the assailant since they were larger than the dead rabbit's feet. Kendra scanned the room but found no other footprints leading further into the house. She guessed the attacker must've left.

A chill slithered down her spine at the thought of what caused such violence. The act seemed primal, yet there was intent behind the mutilation. Jerking her head around, she hoped the creature left.

Kendra, still holding her nose, ran to the kitchen to find cleaning supplies. She didn't want the stench of a dead rabbit to ruin the party.

CHAPTER 12

Ethan observed as his mother set plates on the table. She smiled child-like, with a giggle, which suggested deceptiveness. He felt that she was conspiring a scheme. She seemed too excited for a baby shower that he assumed Lanna didn't want. In text messages, Lanna seemed against raising the baby or celebrating its birth. He wondered if she changed her mind. If so, somehow his mother must've convinced Lanna since Kendra doesn't give up.

Ethan watched as she kept glancing at her phone. He assumed his mother was checking the time or waiting for a message from someone— but who? He figured his mother invited Granny Charlene and Uncle Zek as well. Yet, Uncle Julian said only Lanna, Aunt Chrystal, and everyone at the house would be attending. Ethan rolled his eyes, thinking how the interaction could cause tension. It was obvious from how David acted at Granny Charlene's house.

Ethan watched Uncle Julian crossing his arms and glaring at everyone. Now, Ethan assumed the idea for the party didn't come from his uncle. No, his mother, the mastermind of this event, had planned the party. Ethan hoped his mother wouldn't invite more people. He didn't want to recreate the scene at the store, but he also thought about the shadow that Ayo, the maid, had mentioned. The thought of a creature preying on him, and his family made him feel uneasy.

Bringing everyone together might turn into a bloodbath. The day was sunny enough for a party, but he sensed a storm.

Uncle Julian walked over to Ethan and helped him unfold the chairs. The last decoration left was the banner. Ethan's mother had bought a customized banner that read, *Alanna's Baby Shower*. It seemed over the top, but Lanna might like it. Ethan watched his mother check her phone again. He didn't understand the feeling, but he knew his mother had planned something else.

Glancing at the mini bar, Ethan noticed David avoiding Uncle Julian's gaze. David clenched his jaw and returned to setting up bottles. Ethan never imagined that type of expression on David's face as if someone struck him in the chest. Ethan wondered if David was still upset from those other nights. Ethan would catch them arguing, not too loud, but intense enough to cause concern. He couldn't hear their conversations, but his uncle and David always seemed irritated. He wondered if the tension stemmed from their return from Granny's and Uncle Zek's house. Ethan fidgeted, recalling he had told his uncle their whereabouts. He should've kept quiet.

The thought faded once he noticed Ayo, the maid, bringing a tray of food over to a table. She placed down the food, nodded at him, and went into the house. Ethan recalled having to report to her of anything strange, but he had nothing to share. He only had a feeling, no concrete evidence. After he found the paw prints, the house seemed silent. He didn't feel stalked nor heard claws scraping against walls. In fact, he hasn't had any nightmares either. The silence made him uneasy as if the creature waited to strike. Yet, he tried to trust in the maid and her judgment.

His attention shifted to Lanna and Aunt Chrystal walking into the backyard. Ethan waved at Lanna, but she seemed focused on the baby shower banner. His cousin smacked her lips, twisting them as if she tasted something bitter. Seeing Lanna and Aunt Chrystal, Ethan noticed his mother's strange behavior. He saw the excitement rise on her face.

Lanna swung her head toward Aunt Chrystal. "Ma, is this your idea?"

Aunt Chrystal smacked her lips. "Ain't this what ya wanted?"

"No, I absolutely do not want this, under any circumstances, whatsoever!" Lanna turned toward Ethan, who shrugged and pointed at his mother. Then Lanna turned to Kendra.

"What the fuck is this? You said Lanna wanted this!?" Aunt Chrystal screamed.

Kendra gave a shaky smile. "Um, I thought, and hear me out. We could come together as a family, and you know, discuss some issues."

Before Aunt Chrystal lashed out, Granny Charlene and Uncle Zek arrived. Ethan observed as Julian and David glanced at each other, sharing the same concern. Granny waved at everyone while Zek yawned, his eyes drifting from the scene. Ethan rolled his eyes, realizing he didn't want to be at the party either.

"What y'all doin' here?" Uncle Julian raised a brow.

"You invited me, didn't ya? And, Zek?" Granny folded her arms, shooting a glare at Kendra.

Everyone turned to Kendra, who had a twitchy smile. She attempted to speak but no words came out.

Ethan stood amidst the sudden hush, the backyard an eerie quiet, beside a gust of wind. The trees loomed, branches stirring in anticipation, as if awaiting a storm. Ethan's eyes drifted between the family, his fingers tugging at his shirt. He jerked his head up, as he heard a rumbling above. The ominous sky seemed charged to unleash destruction.

From Lanna's expression, as if witnessing a wolf's jaw open, his guess was correct. His cousin didn't want the baby. His mother must've set up the whole event, including inviting Granny Charlene and Uncle Zek.

Ethan watched as Uncle Julian clenched his fists, and David grabbed a bottle. They both glared at Uncle Zek and Granny Charlene. Now, the uneasiness Ethan felt earlier had intensified. Instead of a creature in the corner of his eyes, he glimpsed Aunt Chrystal taking off her heels.

His mother staggered back, eyes widened as Aunt Chrystal charged. Ethan observed as rage consumed his aunt's face, devouring all reason.

"Chrystal? Chrystal!? Stop!" Kendra cried, shielding herself.

Yet, Lanna flanked from the side, seizing a hand full of hair. His mother's eyes widened as she lost her balance, vulnerable against Aunt Chrystal's fist. His mother's head snapped to the side with a sickening thud that twisted his stomach. He almost wanted to vomit. Instead, he sealed his eyes, refusing to watch anymore. He glimpsed the force of the blow that crumpled her to the ground. Ethan could only watch as his mom bleed on the grass since another fight had erupted in front of him.

Uncle Julian snatched a knife from the table, and thrusted the blade at Uncle Zek, yet cutting the air.

Uncle Zek grinned, snickering as Uncle Julian's jaw tightened.

Uncle Zek stretched out his arms, "Come on Princess!"

Uncle Julian speared the blade again. Yet, with a quick sidestep, Uncle Zek dodged it, hooking his fist into Julian's ribs. Uncle Julian winced, grabbing his side as he stumbled and fell. The knife slipped from his grasp, disappearing into the grass. Uncle Julian should've looked afraid, but his furrowed brows spoke more of annoyance than of fear. Ethan noticed Uncle Julian's vulnerability, and Uncle Zek did too. The man rushed Uncle Julian like a bullet train. Still holding his side, Julian clocked Zek in the face. Uncle Zek cried out and dropped to the ground, aiding Uncle Julian in pinning him down.

Next to them, David was screaming at Granny Charlene. If David hadn't paid attention, her cane would've struck his head and killed him. For an old woman, she could keep up. Even so, she couldn't land a hit on David. Ethan watched as she backed David into a table, pushing him to the ground. Still, Granny Charlene swung her cane, cutting his face, blood splattering the grass. David's arms bled and bruised from fending off Granny Charlene's assault.

Standing in the midst of the confusion, Ethan observed everything. His stomach churned and plummeted, watching them. Everyone was in a rage, and any other human emotion had seemed to disappear from their eyes. Even their bodies moved like puppets. His aunt and cousin had ganged up against his mother while the others were trying to kill each other. This wasn't his family despite their quarrels.

Then, his attention shifted to something moving in the bushes. A fox emerged from the scrubs, snickering as it scanned the chaos. Even in the daylight, its eyes appeared to glow and dance like embers from a flame. It bared its teeth, creating a crooked smile. For a moment, it stared behind Ethan, then cowered back into the bushes. Its fiery eyes disappeared into the shadows of the leaves.

Ethan turned around, Ayo held a stone with weird writings like Egyptian runes. The maid held it up high into the sky.

"STOP!" The Maid's voice resonated through the air, cutting through the tension.

In an instance, everyone stopped, seeming to come out of the trance. The wave of anger that had consumed them had disappeared— at least he hoped. Ethan turned toward the bushes to see if the fox returned but it didn't. He exhaled a heavy sigh, grateful for the fleeting peace.

"Fuck this!" Aunt Chrystal turned from Ayo and stormed out of the backyard. Lanna rushed after her.

"Get out!" Uncle Julian threw a fork at Uncle Zek's feet.

Instead of scowling Zek, Charlene yanked him up, brushing the grass off his clothes. She smacked her lips, examining uncle zek's face. Then, she turned to David; a trickle of blood ran from his forehead to his chin.

Ethan noticed the old lady's eyes had softened, lowering her gaze to the cross around her neck. Then her eyes shifted to the weapon in her hand— a cane.

Granny Charlene looked up, staring at Julian. "Hmm, I allowed hate to fill me." She admitted, her tone gentle.

At this, Uncle Julian raised a brow, standing stiff as he stared at Granny. "Wait!? Did you...?" He asked, lifting his brow more.

Charlene grunted, tugging at Uncle Zek, exiting the backyard. David rolled his eyes, escaping into the house. Kendra, with loose hair tangled in knots, scrubbed the blood from her face. Uncle Julian still stood rigid, trying to finish the first sentence.

Ethan and Ayo shared a glance, a silent understanding passing between them. He sensed that Ayo knew the Shadow's hand in the chaos. The effort to voice his fears and confirm his suspicions had fled, leaving the unknown. Yet, he was certain that they needed to do something— and quick.

Without knowing, the creature may have drained him of his strength. Even family bonds seemed fragile, fading away, but he didn't want to quit the battle. Ethan couldn't stand by and watch his family suffer.

CHAPTER 13

Ethan decided to take a nap. Like before, everything froze. Yet in the dream world, Ethan was at the baby shower. Uncle Julian was mid-strike against Uncle Zek. Lanna and Aunt Chrystal towered over his mother, freezing in frame. He turned his head to the bushes, but the fox wasn't there. Yet, that wasn't the most important change to the scenery. The sky was grey with motionless clouds as if trapped in a painting. He could see the fork of a lightning bolt as it paused in the air before striking the ground. In the backyard, the tables and plates had dust as if laid out for years. Above that, the baby banner had holes as if it had been in a fire. Ethan looked around in hopes to find Ayo, but she wasn't in this dream. The nightmare had seemed to remove everything good or comforting.

Ethan jerked his head to the side. He heard screeching, a twisted chuckle, which he knew came from the fox, but he couldn't see it. Ethan turned to the other side of the yard in search of the creature, where he spotted a tree-like figure.

The leaves were a hue of blood while the trunk stood crooked. Underneath the bark, purple vines pulsed like veins on the rhythm of a heartbeat.

The fox emerged from behind the tree, baring its carnivorous teeth. Its mouth widened, emitting a horrific, ear-piercing sound, as if attempting to speak. Ethan had no doubt this thing was not from his world. The fox's diseased fur hinted at the cloud of toxins from its universe. The grass under its paws began to wither and die.

Ethan gazed upward, beholding the once frozen sky stirring to life. The sky darkened, resembling the first sign of a tornado.

He looked back at the tree and saw the fox had vanished, replaced by something else. The creature's hat gave it the appearance of a scarecrow, like an empty vessel made of hay. Like in a corn field, its eyes, or what he thought were eyes, had followed him. The creature's limbs twisted toward, pointing a jagged claw in his direction.

Ethan blinked and the creature vanished. He searched behind the tree, tables, and bushes, but found nothing like the creature.

Then, claws seemed to grip his spine. He felt its bloodlust on his neck, freezing him in place. Even a glance wouldn't be fast enough before it killed him.

Yet he shifted his gaze, finding curved claws on his shoulder. Closer now, he noticed its hand moved irregularly, like TV static, unstable. As it contorted, a chill urged Ethan to flee. Yet, the entity flickered in front of him, blocking his escape.

The creature opened its jaw, revealing an endless black space. Its mouth, a void, seemed to drag him in while its claw punctured into flesh, leaving a trail of blood down his arms. The pain surged through his muscles like searing flames. He tried pulling away, but the creature had anchored its claws into him. Despite his efforts, he closed his eyes, surrendering death's approach. Ethan figured he couldn't survive since he already cheat death once when he lived instead of his father. His cowardice had materialized his punishment.

Suddenly, the sound of a beast screeched, resonating through the atmosphere. The thunder from above fell silent, ushering in a calmness—a refuge from the terror. Ethan opened his eyes, seeing feathers and a beak, realizing the beast was a white crow. Once more, the small bird gave out a monstrous roar.

The creature jerked its head to the white crow. The bird's aura shined like the sun, causing the creature to tremble. It detached its claws from Ethan's bloody arms, backing away from the crow's divinity. The creature shrieked like a banshee and ran into the shadows of the dream.

The mighty crow flew down, greeting Ethan, who still tried to process the moment. It studied him, with beady eyes, for a while and Ethan almost expected it to speak but it flew away. He had never seen a white crow before. Yet, something seemed familiar about the bird, but Ethan couldn't understand why. He felt this wasn't the first time it protected him.

###

Ethan sat up from his bed. The clock on the wall suggested that he napped for about half an hour. He wondered if his family had calmed down. The silence around him suggested that the fighting had stopped. He heard birds, not a crow, outside his window. Rubbing his eyes, he scanned the bedroom. He sighed with relief, seeing no signs of the shadow or the fox. Ethan tried to stretch, but a stabbing pain shot up his arm. Examining his arms, he saw deep claws marks. He tried to touch the wound, but it stung. Ethan looked under himself to find blood stains on the sheets. He didn't think it could hurt him in real life. Yet, he saw the marks on his arm, which meant the creature and the fox were closer to their world. That's what Ayo would've said. Ethan jumped from his bed, wincing with every movement. Holding his arm, he ran to tell her about his dream.

CHAPTER 14

Lanna slammed the door. Chrystal gripped the steering wheel, turning to her daughter from the passenger's side. Chrystal, who had raised Lanna alone, could tell from her daughter's tensed body that she was about to cry. Although tears didn't trickle down Lanna's face, her eyes appeared to weep. Chrystal assumed Lanna's pained gaze had directed toward Kendra. Chrystal considered dragging Kendra across the backyard again. Yet, she decided that she had caused enough damage. Chrystal made sure her brother's widow wouldn't meddle in people's business again.

Chrystal turned to her daughter in the driver's seat, her head sunk. After the fight with Kendra, her daughter's curls had dropped in tangled knots. When Kendra fell from the fight, she must've grabbed Lanna's hair in an attempt to stay up. If Kendra had hit Lanna in the stomach, Chrystal would've done more than draw a little blood.

As she unclenched her fist, Chrystal gazed at her daughter. She noticed the car keys were in the ignition, but Lanna didn't start the engine. By now, they had been sitting in the driveway for about an hour. Lanna's silence led Chrystal to believe she was upset about the fake party. They could be at home instead of sitting in the scorching car.

"You ain't gonna say nothin'?" Chrystal huffed, waving her hand.

"I can't deal with this drama— all these toxic folks. I'm done!" Lanna's head leaned on the steering wheel.

"Huh?" Chrystal's hand balled into a fist.

She observed as her daughter's body tightened again. Chrystal wondered if Lanna couldn't deal with the family, or with her own mother. From Lanna's side eye, she assumed she meant Chrystal.

If Lanna couldn't do it anymore, the tramp could drop her off and never come back home. Chrystal swung her head away and stared out the window. Alanna Hare had the audacity after Chrystal sacrificed everything for her, *everything*! She didn't understand how her daughter could be selfish— and reckless. Unlike Lanna, Chrystal's mother kicked her out the house by the age of 18 which left no room for carelessness. When Chrystal lived in shelters, she had to take care of a kid who became a constant reminder of those nights. When her daughter was a child, the way Lanna smiled made Chrystal's skin crawl, because that's how he grinned. Her smile asked for a piece of cake while his demanded something else. Chrystal didn't care how it sounded but her daughter reminded her of regrets. She became a pregnant teen who could barely afford a child, not by choice. Yet, Lanna had the option to keep her legs closed. If Chrystal had to carry a baby, why couldn't her prostitute daughter do the same?

Here's what Chrystal concluded, Lanna thought she was mature enough for a baby since she had sex.

Shifting her eyes from the window, Chrystal stared at Lanna's stomach. Chrystal couldn't imagine letting a man invite himself in without protection. In fact, she couldn't even permit a man to touch her.

Chrystal turned her gaze to Lanna's naked shoulders, twisting her lips. Real women don't display their bodies or let men have their way. They act like women...

They act like women.

Chrystal unclenched her fist and looked up at Lanna. She watched as her daughter held a hand to her face, perhaps to conceal the tears or to stifle any words of spite. This expression mirrored her own feelings rather than reminding her of him.

At the dead of night, Chrystal sobbed, convinced her family didn't listen when it mattered.

Her mother didn't believe the man could commit wicked acts which should've been punishable by death. Yet, he was sweet to Charlene, like apple pie, but bitter to Chrystal, like crab apples. For this reason, the girl, an innocent Chrystal, fled to the bathroom. Each visit to the mirror revealed her youth fading away. Mama assumed Chrystal wanted to be grown, but in reality, he was the one who wanted her to act like a woman.

Something seemed familiar about that phrase. An expression her mother had repeated before. The first time Mama said that term was when she was 13 years old and pregnant.

Chrystal rubbed her belly. "I shouldn't have let Kendra talk me into it."

Lanna jerked her head. "She didn't have to! Ever since I was pregnant, you've been judgin' me."

"So, it's my fault? I'm to blame for *you* gettin' pregnant. Well, I didn't ask for this!" Chrystal banged on the dashboard.

"If you didn't want me, then why force me to raise a kid?" Lanna's face twisted and turned away.

Lanna hushed into a silence, looking out the window while her mind seemed to drift away.

Chrystal, too, relapsed into a mute state. She was speechless like those nights he snuck in. Chrystal almost felt herself slip into those memories until she sensed Lanna's gaze on her.

Chrystal's eyes widened at her daughter's lost expression. Chrystal tapped over her face, as if she were afraid of what Lanna's gaze might reveal. With a slow turn, Chrystal faced the side mirror, witnessing the tears fall from her cheeks.

If Chrystal recalled, Lanna had never seen her cry. There were plenty of times she should've shed a tear, but this time she couldn't fight them.

As Lanna sat motionless and gazing, Chrystal covered her face. She couldn't bear the thought of anyone witnessing this kind of vulnerability. She figured Lanna looked at her as if helpless— a victim. Well, she wasn't a victim, she refused to be one. She didn't let anyone run over her. She would never let that happen again.

Chrystal glanced as Lanna's gaze lingered, pausing her breathing. Chrystal huffed at the sight. The ungrateful child had no reason to judge. Her daughter had a choice to let that man inside her, it was Lanna's fault.

"Who's my daddy?" Lanna gazed out the window.

"That don't matter none!" Chrystal rolled her eyes.

Lanna bared her teeth as a tear fell. "It do to me, mama! I wanna meet him...to see what he look like— at least."

Chrystal grinned which caused Lanna to lean in closer as if trying to find the joke. Chrystal watched as her daughter's face twisted into anger, but she felt too exhausted to explain. Telling the truth might make it worse or could stop a cycle of adultery and pain. Chrystal debated back and forth until she made a decision.

"Yah met him already. We went to his funeral…"

"Granddaddy…? Wait, whatcha ya tryin' to say?" Lanna gripped the wheel.

"Don't…! Make me say it out loud. Please…" A tear fell from Chrystal's face.

She turned away from Lanna, finally feeling the heaviness that the truth held. She blinked back tears, holding a cry in her chest. Then, the door slammed, jolting Chrystal out of her thoughts. She turned to an empty seat where Lanna had sat. Chrystal sighed, realizing Lanna had left. It was time, even though she knew her daughter couldn't handle the reality. The truth must've been like swallowing glass.

Chrystal exited the car and found her daughter crouching. She watched as Lanna sobbed into her hands. Rather than feeling the urge to tell her to toughen up, she crouched next to Lanna, gazing at her daughter.

It dawned on Chrystal that her child didn't have the best example of stability. Living with a single mom whose bitterness took hold seemed familiar. As Lanna wept, Chrystal realized that she was no better than her own mother. It seemed that any remaining comfort had shattered from the truth— the bitterness. The cruel truth was that Lanna's grandfather, or father, was a predator.

Unlike her own mother, Chrystal didn't want her daughter to feel alone. All these years she kept the secret because she felt no one would listen. It seemed from the grave that he still held a hand over her mouth. That same hand had found its way to hurting Lanna.

Chrystal placed her hand over her back. Her daughter seemed to fight her mother's touch but soon surrendered.

They rocked for a moment as the blue and red lights came closer to the house. The police cars and an ambulance seemed to be on their way to Julian's house.

Yet, Chrystal thought about how she was going to be different. If she wasn't going to be like her mother, Chrystal had to at least try to understand her daughter.

CHAPTER 15

He scanned the kitchen, finding no sign of Ayo.

Ethan winced, gritting his teeth, as blood stained his fingers where he clutched his arm. Despite the throbbing pain, he rushed into the dining room, but the Maid wasn't there.

Ethan entered the living room, where candles laid across the floor like a cathedral. He watched as Ayo sprinkled rice and white petals on the floor. Under

Ayo's feet were rabbits, mangled and twisted. The rabbit's fur was stuck in something like tar, the same color of the black creature. He almost vomited, seeing guts spilled out on the floor.

After a while she noticed Ethan staring at her and waved for him to join her. He figured she wanted him to help with an incantation. He didn't mind her practice, but he didn't want to partake.

"Don't step on the rabbits. The creature left dark residue on their wounds." Ayo paused, tilting her head, "Eh! What happened to your arm?"

"From a nightmare." Ethan lifted his hand, revealing puncture holes from the creature.

Ayo smacked her lips. "I'm trying to cleanse, but the entity is growing stronger." The Maid went under David's mini bar and grabbed a first aid kit. She cleaned the wound, wrapping it with one of the flower petals. Ethan glanced at her and then at his arm. He noticed in an instant that the throbbing had stopped.

"Thanks..." Ethan said, still gazing at his arm.

Ayo nodded her head toward him, crouching next to one of the rabbits. Ethan noticed she appeared unaffected by the stench. She examined the body as if looking for something small. The Maid held a hand over the rabbit and began humming. Then she opened her eyes and turned toward Ethan.

Ayo took a garbage bag with gloves and started picking up the rabbits. "Tell me about your dream."

"Yeah, sure." Ethan followed Ayo to the fireplace.

He told her, in details, about the dark sky and the tree with bloody leaves. Despite her dumping rabbits into the fire, he continued, knowing she was listening. She paused, squinting at him, as he mentioned the shadow creature trying to eat him. Yet, her raised brow suggested interest in the white crow that protected him.

The Maid wandered around for a bit which made Ethan pace in his spot. He didn't understand what was going on, but he wanted to know.

"We need to banish dis creature before it's too late." Ayo said, writing on a piece of paper, then handing it to him.

Ethan saw that it was a list of items. Strange items he couldn't pronounce and couldn't find in a store. He looked up at her as if asking for help. A certain puzzlement had formed on his face. She must've noticed his concern because her eyes softened.

"Those items should be easy to find. I'm getting the supplies that are harder"

Ethan's shoulders tensed. "Okay…"

The Maid cradled his hand, applying a gentle squeeze. "It's okay… Do as I say to sever its connection to this world, but we must be quick, or more than rabbits will perish in this house."

Ayo also gave him a broom, pointing at the rice and petals. Then she turned back to the fireplace, throwing rabbits in the fire. Ethan nodded, standing tall as he swept the rice and petals into a dustpan.

CHAPTER 16

"Why can't ya leave shit alone!?" Julian shouted in Kendra's face.

Kendra put her foot down. "Don't cuss at me! I wanted to help, but *sorry* for tolerating dysfunction."

David stepped forward. "Kendra, I agree but you went too far. Instead of helping, you made things worse."

Kendra rolled her eyes, snatching a towel from the sink. As she darted into the living room, Julian and David followed. They watched as Kendra began wiping down something dark, resembling tar on the floor.

She grunted, wondering if the maid ever cleaned around the house. Kendra noticed things amiss but didn't see anyone blaming the maid. Yet, Kendra, the one holding everything together, was the issue. It wasn't her fault that the family was in disarray. She's not to blame for Marquis's death— she hoped. She winced, scrubbing harder.

"I've shoulda never listened to ya. What's wrong with ya? Seriously, what's your problem?" Julian raised a brow.

She had bruises and a broken rib from Chrystal and Lanna which kept her quiet. Somehow, she was able to keep herself from crying from the pain. Every inch of her body ached like jagged rocks cutting skin. She needed medical help, but she didn't have insurance. The old house wasn't the only thing she lost after her husband's death.

Despite the pain, Kendra stood up and wiped the shelves, but she didn't look up at Julian. She needed to get her mind off of things.

Julian rushed over to her and yanked the towel from her hand. "Stop it already! That ain't gonna bring'em back."

David stepped in front of Julian. "Enough!"

Kendra hunched over the floor, feeling the failure of cleaning this mess. The situation seemed to overwhelm her. In this case, a garbage bag torn from her grasp, scattering the debris of her life. She longed to gather the shattered pieces and mend her family, but instead, she started a brawl. As a single mother and recent widow, she struggled to keep pace. If Marquis was here, he would know what to do. Tears welled up as her nails dug into her skin, a reminder of her inability to manage without him.

David glared. "Why did you say that? She's trying to cope...and she probably needs medical attention."

"You mean Marquis? He was my family too, but he's dead! Ain't nothin' we can do 'bout that. Besides, she started this mess. Ugh, speakin' of *mess*, we gotta call someone for the backyard." Julian pulled out his phone.

"Forget the backyard! You almost stabbed Zek, your brother. You don't think that's crazy?" David stood in front of Julian with arms folded.

Through her hands, she watched as Julian held the phone from his ear. His brow rose as if looking at David like a stranger. Besides David, Kendra wondered why Julian had a knife in his hand. It was as if Julian always imagined stabbing Zek. She knew the two brothers didn't get along, but she wondered if Julian wanted to kill Zek. Before the baby shower, Kendra would've dismissed the idea. Yet in the fight, Julian didn't hesitate to strike his brother. She wondered if Julian would have stopped or yearned for more violence if he had drawn blood. She prayed he wouldn't, or that she wouldn't have to find out. A chill ran down her spine, hoping Julian wouldn't point the blade at her. Kendra scooted away from Julian but still watched for David's sake.

Julian glanced at David. "Why defend him? No, why are you defendin' everyone else but *me*? You saw what Ezekiel was 'bout to do."

David sighed. "Babe, I'm tired of this. I'm sick of— always convincing my loyalty."

"If it's too much then leave! It ain't like we're married." Julian held the phone to his ear.

"Are you serious?" David's voice rattled as he stepped back.

With tears still in her eyes, Kendra looked up. They must've forgotten she was in the room because it felt as if the conversation wasn't for her ears. From the way Julian ignored David's tears, she guessed this wasn't the first time they had this argument. She watched as Julian headed to the door. David held onto his chest as if something had broken inside. His knees gave away and he fell to the floor. She knew this wasn't right.

"What's *your* problem?" Kendra shouted from the floor.

Julian paused at the door frame, turning to her. "What!?"

"I don't understand how you can push someone away who loves you. The next day isn't promised and I know from personal experience." Kendra held her side, standing up from the floor.

Julian stepped closer to Kendra. "Still can't mind your own business, huh? Fix yourself before ya try to fix someone else."

"I know fixing everything won't bring my husband back, but at least I wasn't afraid to love him." Kendra reached her hand out to David and he took it. He stood up from the floor.

Kendra watched as David marched over to the bald headed man. He only stopped when Julian was about a kiss away. David stared directly into Julian's eyes as if searching for something. Kendra assumed David sought for any love that might've remained. Yet, Kendra wondered if David was wasting his time. She wanted to make a comment about it but from recent events, Kendra decided to leave it alone. Even though she wanted to help, Kendra wanted to see what would happen if she sat back.

David sighed. "Julian hare, we've been together for nine years and you're still the same. I keep believing that you'll change, but I've waited too long. I'm exhausted— sick of this paranoia and excuses." David stood up straight, glaring at Julian, "If you don't decide, I will."

"I…" Julian held his mouth open.

Kendra watched as David waited for more words to come but it seemed he got tired of waiting. She didn't blame David for walking out the room, but she couldn't stare into Julian's eyes. It appeared as if someone had smashed Julian's heart with a hammer. Something cried inside for her to bring David back into the room, but she didn't get involved. Kendra observed as Julian slumped into a chair and his body hunched over. Then to her surprise, he held a hand out to her.

"Please…" Julian's voice rattled.

Kendra stepped back, gripping her pants, wondering what he wanted. Finally, she walked closer, her shoulders tensing with each step. She then slid a chair next to him and sat down. As she did, he reached for her hand. Kendra almost jumped but realized Julian's hands trembled. Kendra found this behavior odd, but then recalled her feelings at Marquis's funeral. She wanted someone by her side, and like herself, Julian didn't want to feel alone. She figured he felt as if he had lost David which might've been true. Although Kendra would argue that David was alive. Meaning Julian had a second chance which most people didn't have. Kendra didn't voice any of these thoughts but rather sat next to Julian as he held her hand.

Someone knocked on the door.

"Open up, it's the police!"

THE FRUIT OF OUR GRIEF

CHAPTER 17

Julian walked into the hallway, seeing blue and red lights. He wondered why the police were at the house. He thought that one of his neighbors was racist enough to call. Then again, someone must've heard the fight from the backyard. Julian ran to the front, placing the chain on the door latch. He wanted to make sure they stayed out. Julian cracked the door open to see an officer. The man in blue held a cloth to his mouth as if about to vomit. Julian noticed the man looked sweaty, almost jittery as he stood by the door frame.

"You the owner of this here home?" The Officer asked.

"Yes, did somethin' happen?" Julian raised a brow.

"Someone done called 'cause they seen some dead rabbits on y'all's front lawn." The Officer gestured for Julian to follow him.

Julian unlatched the chain, trailing behind the cop and stepping on the grass. Like The Officer, Julian recoiled, covering his nose because of the odor that permeated the air. Matted fur, blood, and a substance like black tree sap shrouded the lawn in death. The mangled rabbits were countless with forms contorted in agony. Their torn limbs littered the bushes while their guts dripped from the gate. Above the grim veil, a family of rabbits hung from a tree. Their tongues stuck out and eyes popped from the pressure of the ropes around their necks. Julian felt this was a message, a warning from someone.

His eyes darted around the neighborhood, seeing if someone had their blinds open. He sensed the culprit watching from afar, lurking in the shadows. Yet, no movement proved this paranoia. The houses were quiet, an eerie silence he never heard from this area. He began to ponder the whereabouts of everyone. Even the birds fell into a hush. He turned to The Officer, whose eyes remained vigilant on the scene.

Julian brow rose higher. "What's goin' on?"

"Do ya have any enemies? Or ya know someone who might... uh, do this?" The Officer pointed to the tree of dead rabbits.

Julian handed him the note from his pocket. "A while ago, someone done threw a brick at my window, with a racist note attached. And ain't nobody do nothin', but I ain't surprised."

Kendra ran from the living room. "What happened? Why are the police...?"

Kendra's eyes widened as she surveyed the gruesome scene. David and Ethan rushed outside, joining her by the bushes. As they paused, mirroring Julian's stance, a subtle difference caught his attention. David appeared surprised, while Ethan seemed familiar with such horrors. Julian wondered if Ethan saw the dead vermin inside the house.

"What's going on...?" David stared at the rabbits from the tree.

"A witness done reported somebody vandalizin' this here house. But the suspect was never seen." The Officer sighed.

"Hmm, I've got some suspects for ya. Wait, who saw it?" Julian squinted at The Officer.

Before The Officer answered, Julian noticed Ethan put his headphones on, heading upstairs. Julian figured the family fight and dead rabbits might've overwhelmed Ethan. He didn't blame his nephew for escaping into the house. After seeing the creature in the hallway, Julian felt like curling up in a corner himself. He wondered if someone cursed the house, but also who would have the guts to do it. Would they want to kill him? He could think of several people that hated him, but no one who would want him dead.

Julian had suspicions that the neighbors would terrorize black or queer people. After Mr. Br'er called him a monkey as a joke, Julian swung, reverting back to street rules. Were they ignorant, yes, but destructive or violent… he wasn't sure. At least, not until the broken window incident. He should've ignored David and investigated more of the neighborhood. Their neighbors might be capable of anything.

From behind him, Julian noticed The Maid walked over to join as Kendra followed her son up the stairs. Julian glanced as Kendra's hands trembled, trying to fix her bun. Then he returned his gaze to The Officer.

"Everything alright, sir...?" Ayo tilted her head, her gaze shifting from Julian to the lawn, hardening like ice.

"I'll explain later. Can ya check on Ethan, please? Y'all done got close and he might need a friend."

Julian also wanted to ensure that Kendra didn't further upset the boy. Ayo nodded, stepping back inside, and heading up the stairs. He noticed The Officer trying to enter as well, but Julian blocked his path. The Officer with his head low, backed off, and stood by the bushes.

The Officer cleared his throat. "Who was here at the house?"

"Ya reckon it was one of us?" Julian folded his arms, wondering if Ezekiel trashed his lawn.

"Naw, naw, but we gotta cover every lead." The Officer pulled out a pen and notebook.

Julian sighed as he discussed the party and the attendees, avoiding any mention of the fight. He informed The Officer that his brother and mother had stepped out. Also, his sister and her daughter should've left as well. The Officer took note of this and ended the questions.

"Stay in the house for now. We don't know their motives, yet. I'll be around keepin' watch and collectin' evidence. Backup is also on their way. So don't worry." The Officer nodded his hat and walked away.

Julian wanted to ask more questions, but The Officer was already gone. He wished the police were more helpful. Maybe the cop could call someone to clean up all these dead animals. He paid too much in property taxes for someone to not clean it up.

Julian slammed the door. "Everyone stay in the house until they tell us anything further!"

"Doesn't matter. I'll be in another room. Only disturb me when you want to talk." David side-eyed Julian.

Julian grunted, walking in the other direction from him. He wanted to argue with David, but his body still hurt from fighting Ezekiel. He needed an ice pack and painkillers to stop the throbbing. He should've asked The Officer for a medical team. Yet, he wanted the cop to investigate the yard, not the brawl. Julian decided to head to his office, because that's where he could find medical supplies and peace.

He hoped nothing else disturbed him.

CHAPTER 18

Zek pulled out his phone.

"Hey, I'm here…Okay…Yup, on mah way…"

Zek walked up the stairs.

He made sure to avoid the gum stuck under the railing. After he stepped over a pile of used needles, he observed the building. The neon sign and vintage curtains made the place appear like a 70's retro motel and dull like a cheap tattoo. Places like these usually smelt like cigarettes and stale carpet. Drug dealers hung around these motels such as the man Zek noticed down stairs. The guy had a skull tattooed on his face and something tucked in his hoodie. Zek made sure to not make eye contact in case the man was trigger-happy. Despite the danger, he kept walking down the corridor, wanting to see her. Zek needed to behold *her* beauty again.

He made a quick turn. On his way to 6B, the suite he reserved, Zek heard screaming from a room two doors ahead. With his head down, he rushed past the room. Sometimes it's best to mind your own business. He looked at the time on his phone and realized he was running late.

He stopped at a rusted door with a label that read, 6B. Like Desire had said, the door should've been unlocked. Zek turned the knob and walked into the room. The room was dark with only a few candles.

He saw heels and panties on the floor as the shower ran in the bathroom.

"Hey, ya ready for me?" Zek grinned.

"Gimme a minute. Ya got the cash, suga?" Desire shouted from the bathroom.

"Yeah, sweetheart. All for you!" Zek threw a stack on the bed and sat down.

He felt relieved to escape from everything because that party was a mistake. He wondered why Kendra planned a baby shower for someone who didn't want the baby. It didn't make sense, but that's Kendra. Always meddling in someone's business. She tried that AA meeting shit with him, but he shut that down. Zek figured she needed a man to knock her boots, instead of crying over Marquis. He loved his older brother, but horrible shit happened. Nothing could fix it. Yet, someone should've shot Julian instead of Marquis. Even now, Zek couldn't believe

Julian tried to kill him. Then again, as a kid, Julian was never the same after living on the streets. Something died in Julian a long time ago, but he's always been a sissy. The first time he saw Julian kiss David, he almost vomited. He believed Ethan and Kendra should've found somewhere else to live. At least Ethan would be safer at Mama's house than with those freaks. At the party, he should've done more than punch Julian in the face.

"Put them blind-folds on." Desire shouted from the shower.

"Hmm, we're gettin' a lil adventurous tonight." Zek snatched the blind-fold off the bed.

"Yup, can't wait!"

Zek put on the blindfold. After a few minutes, the water stopped. He heard damp footsteps on the carpet and the bed creaked as someone pressed down.

Then he could smell liquor and tobacco which he knew was her scent. He felt her kiss on his forehead, his cheek and then his lips. He felt hands on him, but they seemed a bit different than what he remembered. Her hands felt tough, almost like a construction worker. He figured the pole made her hands a bit rough. Also, he didn't remember the tobacco smell, but she could have smoked earlier. Zek tried to touch her, but she moved his hand away which he found was weird. He wondered if he did something wrong.

"You alright…?" Zek leaned back.

"Mhmm…" She kissed him on the cheek.

"Somethin' seems…" Zek felt himself flying back on the mattress.

He felt those hands again but around his neck. He never thought she would become this aggressive but here he was being manhandled by her. He wasn't sure if he liked it. He had a sick feeling in his stomach like something was wrong. He tried to push her off him, but she was strong. Now his legs were kicking as she pressed down on his neck. Finally, Zek punched her in the chest and was able to escape. He pulled the blind-fold off. Instead of a beautiful stripper, a huge man stood on top of the bed. The man towered over Zek with hands balled up. Zek couldn't see the man's face, but only a large silhouette.

Zek rushed to the light switch. The fluorescent lights revealed a hairy man, chunky with a devilish look. The man wore fishnets and a dress with lipstick. Despite the clothes and makeup, he remembered that face because it was his father. Yet, none of it made sense. His father was dead. Zek thought someone had drugged him, but the tobacco smell and those hands felt too real. They were cold like his stare, forcing their way into his thoughts. The father imposter grinned, sensing Zek's fist tremble.

Zek stumbled back, colliding with the closet, then hearing a thud at his feet. His eyes widened, staring at a corpse in a fox mink coat. Her body contorted like tree roots, her neck bearing raw marks from the tight grip of a rope. He glanced at Desire's body, her empty sockets, then turned away, vomiting on the carpet. When he looked up, he saw the imposter jumping off the bed, grinning at its project.

The imposter sat down, patting the bed. "Sit next to me, son."

Zek wanted to resist but an old instinct told him to obey. He sat down on the bed, farthest away from the imposter. Zek looked down, realizing he soiled himself.

"How…?" Zek gripped the covers.

"Ya know I love ya, son, right?" the imposter began to take his shirt off.

"You're...you should be dead..." Zek leaned back.

The imposter grinned. "Mhm, come closer."

Zek stood up, shaking. "No..."

"I SAID COME HERE!" The imposter's voice, unlike anything he heard before, sounded cold and detached.

Ezekiel stayed, feeling the urine drip down his leg. Then, it charged him. Somehow his body moved, dodging the attack. He needed to leave. He wasn't sure what was going on, but it felt more dangerous than his real father. Zek rushed to the door, but the imposter jumped in front of him. The thing walked toward him with claws. Zek jumped back, realizing it had eyes like hellish flames. He balled up his fist, but he wasn't sure if he could throw a punch.

He froze like when he was a kid— helpless. His lip bled as he broke skin, looking away from the imposter. He wondered why he felt this way. Yet, an old memory, stripping and revealing secrets, reminded him. He recalled car rides to Pa's special spot, somewhere mama wouldn't bother their bonding time. This didn't mean fishing, shooting game, or other activities that dads and sons usually did in the south. "Bonding time" meant things to not tell others, and boys don't cry. This was a lie Pa told him as he unzipped his innocence and stanched it away. The naked truth was that Pa found pleasure in calling Zek his princess, his conquest. Zek produced a jittery laugh, recalling Julian's stupid face. Zek didn't want his lifestyle, but his pride. He was jealous that his little brother was safer in the streets than at home. Even as he watched the imposter, Zek felt its eyes grope him like Pa.

"Go sit down on the bed, NOW!" The imposter clawed the door, leaving huge marks in the metal.

"N-no…" Zek's lip quivered as the words came out like tears.

The imposter rushed Zek again. Out of instinct, Zek grabbed the closest thing to protect himself— a candle. He wanted to grab something else, but his arms locked up, hands gripping around the wax. He shut his eyes, hearing heavy steps charge at him.

Then, Zek heard silence, opening his eyes he saw claws frozen in mid-air. It seemed the creature had tried to go through an invisible wall. Zek noticed the creature was staring at the candle. He wondered if the candle scared the thing. Zek held out the flame, watching as it winched back. With a deep breath, Zek stepped forward, pushing the creature back. Unlike when Zek was small, he could finally stand his ground. He felt like the man he always wanted to be, not what

Pa tried to mold him into. He wasn't his mother's and siblings' disappointment. No! Zek was a man, not the drugs, sex, and abuse. He didn't need to prove his strength; he was strong enough. The imposter fell back until Zek got to the door. He swung the door and then slammed it. Zek ran as fast as he could, covering the candle with his hand so the flame wouldn't go out.

CHAPTER 19

Charlene, like a raging bull, approached the door. Her knuckles hit the wood on repeat, until they turned purple. As she waited, she observed the devilish scene.

Across the lawn she saw blood staining the leaves and seeping into the roots. In the Mississippi breeze, the critters swung. Strange hares with matted fur and twisted mouths hung from trees.

She wondered who would do something so sinister. Charlene jumped, turning to the sound of a click as Julian emerged from the door.

His mouth opened to speak but she huffed, pushing him aside. Charlene didn't care to hear him complain. If Julian wanted to call the cops, then he could walk outside and get them himself. She needed to find Ezekiel. She sensed he was in danger, her mother's intuition kept yanking at her to find him. She ran around the house, looking for her son, and screaming Zek's name.

Charlene ran up to Julian. "What ya do to Zek!?"

"He ain't here. Did ya call him?" Julain folded his arms.

"Yes, but he ain't answerin' mah calls. He ain't home either, so he can't be anywhere else but here. Wait, why them cops outside? Somebody done died?

My baby dead!?" Charlene looked out the window, trembling with tears.

Julian grunted, moving toward the door. "It was them dead rabbits. Not Ezekiel, sadly." Julian sighed, watching tears fall from the old lady's face, "Stay inside. The cops ain't caught the person who done this. Also, I don't want your dead body stinkin' up my yard."

Charlene rolled her eyes, then exhaled. "Y'okay? Someone tryna hurt ya?"

Julian raised a brow, then squinted. "Stay down stairs and don't go into my office."

Charlene twisted her lips, marching her way toward Julian in protest. Yet, Chrystal and Lanna rushed through the door, blocking her path. If it wasn't for Chrystal and Lanna, she would've smacked the taste out of his mouth.

"Why them police outside?" Chystral stared at the curtains shifting from blue to red.

Julain sighed. "Someone..."

Everyone turned their heads toward the back of the house as something crashed. The house went silent as they listened. Then again, another crash had shattered the silence.

Julian darted to the closet, grabbing a rifle. As he walked in the direction of the sound, Chrystal and Charlene trailed him. Charlene turned around, noticing Lanna had sat down, clutching her head. She figured her granddaughter had nausea from the baby. It might be best for her to stay behind.

Charlene turned back around, seeing they were entering a room.

In the dim light, Charlene could make out the shape of boxes and old furniture. Further in the dark, she heard shuffling, and spotted a faint glow. She couldn't see the face, but the silhouette of a man emerged, creeping its way toward them. As Charlene stepped back, Julian aimed the rifle while Chrystal grabbed a bat.

The black figure came closer, revealing a small flame from a candle. The light revealed the figure's face as Ezekiel.

Chrystal held her nose. "You done pissed yourself?"

"Shut up, Chrystal! Anyone would piss themselves if a gun was pointed at 'em. Why's it so dark in here!?" Zek turned around, scanning the darkness.

Charlene squinted at Zek, noticing his vilgeance, wondering what he was searching for. She thought he appeared sober but not mentally well. He displayed a type of fear she hadn't seen since he was a child. He looked distressed. Paranoid. He scanned the darkness as if waiting for something to snatch him. She watched as Zek fidgeted with the candle.

With a candle in his hand, Zek raised his hands in a surrender pose. Julian kept the rifle pointed at Zek until Charlene pushed down the barrel.

"Whatcha doin' in here?" Julian raised a brow.

"Don't worry. Oh! Thanks for not shootin' me." Zek looked behind the group, "Why them cops here?"

"I thought the police was here for you. Where ya been? I been worried sick, I was thinkin' somethin' terrible done happened!" Charlene ran over, hugging Zek. Yet, she could feel his body tense from her touch. She pulled back from the hug, staring into his eyes. "Y'okay, sweetheart?"

"Um, ya don't gotta worry, but thanks, Ma?" Zek mumbled, stumbling back.

"Doesn't matter. I want ya outta the house, Ezekiel. Actually, all y'all can leave, now!" Julian huffed, pointing to the front door.

Charlene grunted, glaring at Julian. She wondered if he was still upset from the party.

Despite her frustration, they all headed to the front. Zek grabbed the knob, but it wouldn't turn. Chrystal rolled her eyes and pushed him out the way. She tried as well but the door didn't budge.

"What's wrong with y'all's stupid door?" Chrystal jerked her head toward Julian.

"Nothin', it should open." The knob didn't turn for Julian either. Even after he unlocked it, the door didn't move.

"Hey, where are we...?" Lanna said, looking through the curtains.

Chrystal smacked her lips. "Huh...? We in Mississippi, girl. You done hit ya head?"

Lanna rolled her eyes and waved everyone to the window. Once everyone got to the glass, Charlene understood Lanna's confusion. The outside of the house was an alien void. Not like the ghastly eyes of stars and galaxies, but a darkness that swallowed light. The void consumed everything beyond the iron gates, as they floated in a sea of twilight.

Charlene withdrew from the window, feeling safer inside than in that other world. Her mind couldn't comprehend the situation nor predict her family's fate.

CHAPTER 20

The house went pitch-black. Ethan heard someone flipping the light switch, but the room stayed dark. Then, a candle sparked to life with Uncle Zek holding it.

They stood in what seemed to be the living room. Mold crawled on the ceiling like insects. The walls bled a substance like tar, oozing downward. Ethan recoiled, seeing the tar bubble and hiss like lava.

From this distance, it smelled rotten like dead rodents. He recalled the mangled rabbits, turning his head, he stopped himself from vomiting.

His mother, Kendra, gripped David's arm while Lanna sat in the chair next to them, still nauseous. David clutched Kendra's hand, his eyes seeking familiarity in this foreign space.

As the tar crept on the floor, they all huddled around Granny Charlene folding her arms. Ethan figured from Granny's expression, she was processing the situation.

Next to his grandmother, Uncle Julian scanned the room, noticing the sizzling tar. Uncle Julian gripped his gun while next to him Ayo pulled items from her apron. She mixed and ground her ingredients into vials. She seemed unfazed from how her gaze fixated on her potions instead of the walls.

Ethan eyed Uncle Zek clutching the candle as if his life hung on it. Ethan didn't think a draft could blow through the locked windows since nothing could come in or out.

Ethan turned, watching Aunt Chrystal pick up a chair, slamming it on the window but the glass didn't crack. Yet, he saw the chair broken into splintered pieces. Even after her first attempt had failed, Aunt Chrystal grabbed a vase.

"Don't…!" Uncle Julian yanked the vase from Aunt Chrystal.

"Move…!" Aunt Chrystal pushed him and grabbed another chair.

"Chrystal, never mind…I'm goin' to the basement. Them lights ain't turnin' on by themselves." Uncle Julian opened a drawer.

Uncle Julian pulled out two candles and a lighter. He held out the second candle to David, but he didn't take the candle, rather he turned away, balling his fist.

Ethan assumed something happened between the two. He watched as Uncle Julian reached out to David, then paused, retracting his hand. Uncle Julian's shoulders sagged, his jaws clenching under a silent weight.

With an exhale, he turned away, stepping into the darkness alone. Ethan observed as David stood facing the walls, folding his arms.

Ethan jerked his head to the sound of wood snapping. More pieces of a chair scattered across the floor, but the window didn't have a scratch. Aunt Chrystal dragged a chair from the dining room.

Kendra stepped in front of Aunt Chrystal. "Maybe you…"

"Maybe what…? Maybe, you should shut up!" Aunt Chrystal yanked Kendra by her hair.

The two women began rolling on the floor like feral animals. Aunt Chrystal clawed out a chunk of his mother's hair while Kendra rammed her fist into his aunt's face. Ethan's mother kept slamming her fist, but his aunt appeared too enraged to feel the blood. Yet, they froze, hearing a low bellow from the darkness. A voice, deep as the ocean's depths, started to chuckle. Aunt Chrystal and his mother shot up from the floor. Ethan's eyes jolted to the corners of the room, but he didn't see anything. In hope for answers, Ethan turned to Ayo who seemed fixated on the hallway. The hall was dark, but Ethan could see something black tower over The Maid. Its crooked fingers clawed into the frame of the door as Ayo inched back. It would've stood above seven feet tall if its spine didn't twist like a serpent. Red eyes as if flames stared at The Maid. It appeared Ayo was pulling something from her apron. Ethan blinked and then The Maid's head toppled to the floor. The shadow's claw dripped with blood while its laughter oozed with wickedness. Still staring at her head, Ethan dropped to the floor. He couldn't believe what he was seeing. Everything happened at the speed of a bullet. The only person he told how he felt the day his father died was now a body and a head. He alone understood the depth of this defeat, for Ayo sought vengeance for her father's murder. She could never have that.

His focus stayed on the decapitated head and the world around him turned fuzzy. He couldn't feel his heartbeat but that didn't seem to matter because they were going to die. He wasn't going to cheat death this time.

Lanna's scream snapped him out of his shock. From behind him, his mother ran over and lifted him to the opposite direction of the creature. Once she dragged him to safety, Ethan noticed David trying to calm Lanna. Aunt Chrystal grabbed a wooden piece from the broken chairs and charged the shadow. Regardless of his aunt's attempt, the shadow flicked her to the wall. Her body slammed the floor, unmoving from her spot. Ethan thought Aunt Chrystal looked dead. His mother rushed over to Aunt Chrystal and hauled her over to them. From her pulse, David claimed she was alive but knocked out. It didn't matter because they couldn't stop this thing.

Ethan glanced at the dead stare in Ayo's eyes. The only one who knew how to banish this creature was a corpse.

Uncle Zek jumped in front of them. He stretched out the candle toward the creature. Ethan wondered what he was doing but noticed the creature's form appeared to flicker. Its body coiled back into the dark hallway. Its blazing eyes seemed concentrated on the light in Uncle Zek's hand. Ethan pondered if the flame scared the shadow, an unknown weakness. Ethan watched Uncle Zek advance, as the creature slithered back into the darkness. A smile raised on Ethan's face, realizing they might have a chance. He watched his uncle walking forward until the creature disappeared. Uncle Zek came back over to the group, seeing the shadow was gone for now.

He wanted to yell at David, tell him that he was over dramatic. Yet, he wanted to say… sorry, to atone for his selfishness. Julian criticized people's motives but somehow acted as the ones he scorned. Julian clutched the rifle, then softened his grip. He sighed, knowing he needed to turn on the lights first.

Julian searched through the drawer. He found a flashlight which he kept for emergencies. Yet, when he clicked the button, it failed to turn on. He assumed nothing electrical worked in the house. He kept the candle and lighter instead. Julian opened the door to the basement. To his surprise he didn't need the candle because there was light down the steps. In the basement, the red glow was like flames but didn't move as wild. Instead, the glow seemed to pulse on the rhythm of a beating heart. He wondered if a fire melted the wires in the power box. Even so, the temperature from the basement didn't scorch his skin. As he descended the stairs, he shivered, the cold seeping into his bones. He could even see his breath.

Once he stepped on the bottom of the stairs, there was a tree with red leaves and a twisted trunk. Something that looked like fruit hung from the branches. The bizarre fruit pulsed like a heart and a black liquid oozed from its skin. He could hear gnats flying around the fruit which also smelt rotten. Julian wanted to cut it down but doubted its effectiveness. The bark of the trunk looked like ff type of obsidian.

Also, he thought about one of those fruits bursting. He didn't want to gamble if the juices wouldn't melt his face.

Julian looked up the stairs. He doubted David's help due to past regrets but trusted the others to listen. Julian ran up the stairs.

Lanna was the first to see the strange tree. Her eyes widened as the tree hummed its foreign tune. Aunt Chrystal and Kendra seemed to notice the grotesque fruit. They watched as the pods pulsed and oozed a black sap on the branches. Next to the two women were Uncle Zek, Granny Charlene, and David. The three of them stared at the bruised purple trunk which appeared cracked and dull. Everyone gazed at the tree, and that's if it was a plant. Without question, they knew this thing wasn't from this world.

"I've seen this before." Ethan said.

Every eye turned toward him, fixing in a gaze of puzzled dread. They all shifted into a rigid posture, exchanging glances between each other.

Ethan lowered his head, realizing it was time. He explained the details of his nightmares, watching as their eyes widened. Following his lead, his mother, David, and Julian shared their strange encounters. This prompted everyone else to share their experiences both in and out the house.

Amidst the conversations, Ethan's mind faded into panic. While sharing stories felt comforting, escape without Ayo seemed impossible.

CHAPTER 21

"How are we supposed to get out?" Kendra looked at the others.

"I thought ya woulda had a plan. Or you're only good at plannin' fake parties?" Aunt Chrystal rolled her eyes.

Kendra smacked her lips. "Please, shut up! Being bitter won't make you prettier."

"Let's not fight…" David slumped on the floor with his head lowered.

Aunt Chrystal glared at David as if pondering to smash the window upstairs or his face. David growled in return, directly staring at her. Ethan wondered if being in the basement or feeling trapped in the house was what made David and Aunt Chrystal on edge. He watched as his aunt balled up her fist, only to release it moments later. Ethan assumed she was still dizzy from the knock-out.

"I'm gonna hurt him, Julian. Get him!" Aunt Chrystal snarled.

"Chrystal, everyone is tired and irritated— not just you. And it's not like he would care anyway." David side-eyed Uncle Julian.

This sparked an argument between everyone in the group. David screamed at Uncle Julian while his mother began yelling at Aunt Chrystal.

Lanna slammed a bottle on the floor, shattering it into pieces. Aunt Chrystal paused, gasping, as Lanna marched up to his mother. His cousin started cussing her out, with his aunt joining in.

Ethan watched the brewing brawl until he noticed the shift in the basement. The room became darker as they argued and the fruit from the tree began to pulse with excitement. Ethan tried to show everyone the fruit, but no one listened, not even his mother, who seemed to be in a trance. After a minute, Ethan felt an urge to rip someone apart, destroying everything in the house. His vision narrowed to a blurry tunnel, as if underground. He almost gave in until Granny Charlene pushed him aside. Somehow that broke the tree's hypnosis. Ethan observed as Granny stood sturdy like a statue.

"What's wrong with y'all? Get it together!" Granny Charlene shouted.

Everyone paused, engulfed in a long, almost endless silence. Only the hum from the tree reverberated in the room. The silence wasn't due to Granny Charlene shouting but rather a feeling. Ethan wasn't sure if everyone else felt it, but something made his skin crawl, urging him to run. Instead, he and the others stared at the corner.

From the shadows emerged a fox with gray fur. It smiled at them, revealing fangs. Its eyes illuminated an ominous hue while its mouth curled in a crooked angle as it gazed at the family. In unison, they backed up from the fox. Behind the creature, the sound of a bell rang, as if submerged underwater. The fox turned its head like an owl, facing that direction.

A black figure emerged from the darkness. Its crooked limbs and body twisted in unnatural ways. The shadow towered over the fox and looked down at them. Ethan could feel the bloodlust oozing from its devilish eyes. This creature wasn't going to stop at killing The Maid but willing to consume his entire family. Ethan noticed the fruit pulsed as if in sync with the creature. When the creature appeared to breathe the fruit expanded like lungs. Ethan recalled Ayo mentioning the shadow would have a connection to this world. It's possible the weird fruit was that link.

"I have a plan." Ethan turned, whispering to the group.

Julian raised a brow. "I'll listen. What ya thinkin'?"

Ethan waved everyone in to get closer. He wanted to ensure they all heard, knowing time was running out before the shadow would attack. The plan was for Uncle Julian, Uncle Zek, and David to distract the creatures. Then, the others would make Molotov bombs from David's liquor storage. Last, they burn the tree, severing the creatures' connection to this world.

Everyone glanced at each other as if hesitant but there didn't seem to be another way to kill a shadow.

"Sounds good to me. You take the lead." Kendra looked amongst the group, but no one disagreed.

As everyone dispersed, Uncle Zek's movements became deliberate and precise. He lit each candle with a steady hand, passing them out one by one. Ethan's uncles shared a glance, nodding as they traded items, a silent truce between the two. Then, Uncle Julian turned to David, offering him a candle. David paused, inhaling deep, before accepting it.

The three men held out the candles as planned, giving the others time to work on Molotovs. As they worked, Ethan glanced at the shadow and fox, noticing the creatures inching back. The plan seemed effective. Ethan resumed their task, observing Granny Charlene's flawless execution. He wondered when she learned this skill, or why she would need it.

Ethan turned to the shadow which towered over the men. "It's still big. I don't know if they can defend long enough."

Lanna placed a Molotov next to Ethan. "It's fine, we're almost done. And, I gotta plan."

Ethan nodded, returning to working on the weapons. He didn't know what Lanna had planned, but there wasn't time to ask. The candles were getting shorter. After finishing the last Molotov, Granny Charlene and him snuck behind the creatures.

David's hands trembled as he faced the distorted figure. Its eyes flared as if in an infernal blaze, staring at the three mortal men. David looked at his candle, the wax melting, shrinking as it repealed the creatures. David shifted his gaze from shadow to the foxlike beast creeping closer.

"Hey…" Julian tapped him.

David sighed. "Yeah? Kind of busy right now."

"Um, well— ugh." Julian exhaled, "I-I'm sorry…"

David glanced at Julian, then kept his eyes on the snarling fox. He noticed as the candle reduced in size, the fox shoved back.

"Sorry you can't fool me anymore? Or, that you wasted my time?" David rolled his eyes.

"Can y'all stop that bickerin'? Y'all makin me wanna get high." Ezekiel fidgeted with the candle.

David smacked his lips. "It's not my fault he waited nine years to realize what he had."

Julian sighed, mumbling something under his breath. Ignoring the comment, David noticed Julian's candle melted faster. He wondered how long before the creatures would rip them apart.

"Both of y'all ain't right." Ezekiel cleared his throat, "Julian, I understand the feelin' of broken trust. Someone who shoulda loved ya, but exploits instead. Yet, that ain't David. Trust me, the dude is a goody-two-shoe. If anythin', me and the rest of the family are all messed up in the head." Ezekiel's voice seemed to rattle, a subtle emotion that David sensed.

"Hmm, it seemed your brother noticed before you." David smirked.

Ezekiel wiped his eyes. "Aye, shut up! You shoulda spoke up for yourself. No one forced ya to stay. I didn't! He didn't! But, you did. It was all you! So, since ya plan on hangin' around, man up, right? Listen, this prostitute told me 'bout settin' boundaries or somethin' like that. If we survive, I'll give ya her number."

David nodded, clenching his jaw, hating to admit that Ezekiel might've been correct. No one pointed a gun at his head, telling him to commit, or else. Yet, he remained, keeping everything inside, for nine years. No, his entire life. Even outside of the relationship, he wanted the world to shine gold. As he stared into the darkness ahead, he wondered if the same deep rage lurked within him, repressed. Something inside himself waiting to ignite, burning everything in its path.

David watched the flame burn the wick, feeling the heat on his fingers. In front of the them, the creatures were almost slashing distance. He exhaled, releasing the tension from his shoulders, staring at Julian. Before they died, he needed to speak his mind.

"If we continue this…" David glanced at the creatures, "If we live, I need to see more trust. No guards and no walls. Also, you're right, the neighbors are racist. We should move."

"Okay." Julian nodded.

"Aw, shit, I need a blunt! Ha-ha! Kiddin'— a little bit..." Ezekiel's candle was now a stub.

Julian raised a brow. "If we make it out, I'm gonna pay for your rehab."

Lanna turned toward her mother. "You gotta be nice to Aunt Kendra"

Chrystal smacked her lips. "Why I gotta?"

"Ethan suggested we swap out that negative energy it feeds on." Lanna watched as her mom and Aunt Kendra stared at each other.

Aunt Kendra's mouth twisted as she felt around her head where Chrystal yanked the hair out. In return, Lanna's mama held her face where Aunt Kendra left nail marks. They both glared at the other which made Lanna question the effectiveness of the plan.

Lanna, rubbing her pregnant belly, tapped her mother, reminding her of the promise she made. Her mama, Chrystal, will be a better mother. Lanna watched as her mother's eyes soften. Lanna turned to Aunt Kendra, hugging her as a way to apologize for the violence against her own kin. Lanna didn't understand what prompted her to act so vicious toward her aunt. It could've been the creature, a deep hatred she was unaware of, or both. Either way, her actions were unacceptable.

Lanna, Aunt Kendra, and her mother turned toward the other worldly things in the basement. By this time, if they were going to survive, those two needed to get along.

Kendra rolled her eyes. "I'm sorry, I wanted to help but, um, I might've—No, I made mistakes." Aunt

Kendra stared at the creatures, "And, right now, I'm frightened. I don't know how to fix this." She muttered, her voice quivering.

"My bad too. I'm…" Chrystal exhaled, wiping her eyes. "I'm dealin' with a lot right now, well, I've dealt with it for a long time— in silence. Bottled up. Swelling like a blister. And, I don't know how to fix it which scares me too." Chrystal sniffled.

Aunt Kendra leaned in. "I won't ask, but I'm here."

Her mother nodded, wiping her face. With a slow tap on the back, her mother embraced Aunt Kendra's hug.

Lanna watched as her mama and Aunt Kendra held hands then they reached for hers. Lanna smiled as they began chanting compliments. At first, it felt awkward, a little silly, but it seemed to work. The shadow shrunk a bit and turned a dark gray. Looking closer, Lanna noticed its body was almost transparent. Near the shadow, the eyes of the fox seemed to dim instead of the blaze they once had.

Even though their candles were almost a wick, Lanna watched as the men pushed the creatures back in unity. Her plan was working! Now, Ethan and Granny Charlene had to do the rest of his plan.

While the women weakened the creatures, Granny Charlene and Ethan snuck behind it. Despite their efforts, the shadow jerked its head toward Ethan. Fear paralyzed him as its claws towered over him, intent on killing.

Right as the creature lunged, almost ripping into flesh, Granny Charlene shielded him. His eyes widened as his grandmother hit the floor.

Ethan rushed to her, but she signaled for him to stop. She seemed too weak to speak but she mouthed for him to throw it.

Ethan glanced at the Molotov and then his grandmother. He wanted to bring her back to the group, but he feared the shadow might attack again.

Ethan glanced at the twisted tree, seeing it pulsed a wicked red. He couldn't do it.

"Ethan... don't be... scared, darlin'", Granny Charlene gargled, "You're my grandson, a child of God which means you shouldn't fear."

As the blood stained her shirt, tears began to run down her face. "I blames myself for your daddy's death and the family's troubles. I done failed to protect 'em, till now, but you can. I believe in you, baby."

He didn't want anyone to die because of him. His father died protecting him; now his grandmother risked the same.

Ethan watched as his grandmother's body appeared fragile, but her eyes were steady as a mountain. Somehow, they gave him confidence.

He turned, gripping the bottle tighter as he stared at the shadow.

He despised this feeling. The same sensation when the killer shot his dad while Ethan hid. This creature, a calamity of death, influenced the ugliness in his family. It feed on his insecurities— and theirs as well. All this violence and anxiety made him nauseous. He couldn't live like this anymore. He wanted to fight back. His grandmother was right, he needed to protect his family. Ethan took a lighter and lit the cloth.

He stared at the tree, seeing that it was only the fruit of this evil, their bickering and grief. As Ethan looked back, it seemed malice was his father's killer. Even now, He saw a resemblance in the tree's aura to the murderer's eyes— inhuman. A sight devoid of reason, contorted like these twilight beings.

With tears in his eyes, Ethan hurled the bottle at the tree. It ignited, a quick fierce blaze, heating the air. While from its branches, the fruit burst and splattered across the walls of the basement. In response, the fox went ablaze as well, melting into a puddle of bubbling tar.

The shadow shrieked in pain, watching its creation turn to ashes and tar. It twitched, retreating into the dark space of the room. Once it left, Ethan noticed the air felt lighter as if something stepped off his chest.

Everyone ran over to Granny Charlene as she clutched her stomach, her guts spilling out. Ethan observed his mother weeping over Granny, while Aunt Chrystal's eyes welled up. David and Lanna embraced Julian as he trembled, leaning over the old woman.

Again, Ethan felt that this was his fault. He survived once more but at a cost. If Granny died, they may never forgive him.

Granny Charlene looked up at them. "It ain't your fault...it's mine. I'm the one that shoulda been a better mama."

Ethan took his grandmother's hand. "It's my fault..."

"No! I did what I had to do to protect you...same as your daddy, Ethan. As a parent, I shoulda protected my children more." Granny Charlene glanced at Aunt Chrystal, Uncle Julian, and Uncle Zek

Uncle Zek leaned closer. "Ma, I'll be better... I'll clean up the house more, I-I'll stop the drugs, but don't die on us, please."

Granny Charlene held Uncle Zek's hand. They all watched as Granny Charlene tried to position herself up. Ethan's mother crouched, holding one side while Uncle Zek helped with the other arm. They put her back on the wall. The old woman seemed to stare at them as if gazing at a sunset. Ethan noticed her eyes began to water but she held the tears back with a sniff. Ethan assumed this was not for selfish reasons but to make sure everyone wouldn't worry about her.

Granny Charlene tightened her grip on Uncle Zek's hand. "Everythin' gonna be alright, darlin'. Don't fight among each other, ya hear?" She scanned the group, making sure they all nodded in agreement.

They all seemed to accept the term. Ethan turned to the burning tree. He stared until the fire had died down into ashes. His gaze returned to his grandmother, but life had departed from her eyes. Her body went limp as her hand had loosened from Uncle Zek's grip. In the moment of sudden loss, his aunt and uncles clung together. The siblings seemed to embrace what had remained of the family, since losing a brother and a mother. Ethan enveloped his mother as her body quivered in his arms. He knew his mother and granny didn't get along, but they never hated each other. Even David held Lanna, both who wasn't fond of the old lady, weeped together. Everyone had endured loss, and pain they didn't speak of, but they might've gained as well. Ethan felt he had developed a strength he never knew. As he scanned the people around himself, he found a fortress within his family.

From the basement window, the morning light came through. Ethan could see his grandmother's ghost-like skin in the light. From the glass, a white crow cawed from outside. An old white crow that appeared to have sturdy wings and steady eyes, staring at them. Ethan felt his dad was still watching over him, but Granny Charlene was as well.